Now...a
Harlequin
romance
by Anne Mather
comes to life
on the movie screen

starring
KEIR DULLEA · SUSAN PENHALIGON

Leopard in the Snow

Guest Stars
KENNETH MORE · BILLIE WHITELAW

featuring GORDON THOMSON as MICHAEL
and JEREMY KEMP as BOLT

Produced by JOHN QUESTED and CHRIS HARROP
Screenplay by ANNE MATHER and JILL HYEM
Directed by GERRY O'HARA
An Anglo-Canadian Co-Production

WELCOME
TO THE WONDERFUL WORLD
OF *Harlequin Romances*

Interesting, informative and entertaining,
each Harlequin Romance portrays an appealing
and original love story. With a varied array
of settings, we may lure you on an African safari,
to a quaint Welsh village, or an exotic riviera
location—anywhere and everywhere that adventurous
men and women fall in love.

As publishers of Harlequin Romances we're
extremely proud of our books. Since 1949,
Harlequin Enterprises has built its publishing
reputation on the solid base of quality and
originality. Our stories are the most popular
paperback romances sold in North America; every
month, eight new titles are released and sold at
nearly every book-selling store in Canada and the
United States.

A free catalogue listing all available Harlequin Romances
can be your by writing to the

HARLEQUIN READER SERVICE,
(In the U.S.) M.P.O. Box 707, Niagara Falls, N.Y. 14302
(In Canada) Stratford, Ontario, Canada   N5A 6W4

or use order coupon at back of books.

We sincerely hope you enjoy reading
this Harlequin Romance.

Yours truly,

THE PUBLISHERS
  Harlequin Romances

Kim Harman

Wife to Charles

by

SOPHIE WESTON

Harlequin Books

TORONTO • LONDON • NEW YORK • AMSTERDAM • SYDNEY

Original hardcover edition published in 1977
by Mills & Boon Limited

ISBN 0-373-02129-1

Harlequin edition published January 1978

PRINTED IN U.S.A.

CHAPTER ONE

THERE was an intimidating silence. At least one of the girls left facing each other across the large oak desk found it intimidating. What the other felt was not easy to guess. Her cool grey eyes surveyed her sister without expression.

'Well?' she demanded. She tilted her heavy executive chair back at a dangerous angle against the window-sill and waited.

Patience, reflected her sister not a little resentfully, had always been one of Becky's greatest failings. It had taken her doggedly through university and the legal examinations that she had found so difficult. It had turned her into one of the most successful assistant solicitors that James Lord's country practice had ever housed. And when she left the practice and England for the legal division of the English delegation to the European Parliament it had helped her to support the vagaries of her masters and the slow processes of the machine for which she worked with exemplary equanimity. Now she sat quietly and waited for Chloe to speak.

'Oh, Becky, I'm sorry,' Chloe blurted out in real consternation. 'I had no idea it would be so difficult to get in to see you.'

'But you haven't found it difficult,' pointed out her sister with justice. 'You're here.'

Chloe hung her head.

'Against all regulations, I may say,' pursued her sister inexorably.

'I just sort of walked in.'

'So I gather,' replied Becky austerely. She looked at her

sister's lowered head and her lips twitched. 'You do realise that the messengers are quite convinced you're a spy? And that I'm in league with you? There could well be a diplomatic incident.'

Chloe judged it better to make no reply to this. She had, in fact, been rather taken aback at the consternation she had caused by walking into the Parliamentary building in Strasbourg and demanding to see Miss Summerson. For a moment she had been quite afraid of what might happen to her as an assortment of security officers had gathered about her quaking form, insisting that nobody, but nobody, entered the building without prior authorisation. Clearly Becky, at whose name they had moderated their tones and agreed to consult the English delegation before hauling Chloe off to detention, was a personage of more importance than her sister had been quite prepared for.

'Not only me,' pursued Miss Summerson, 'the whole division. John Townsend in particular, as he's the head of it.'

Chloe relaxed at the familiar name. She had met Mr Townsend on a couple of occasions in London and liked him. She had also formed the shrewd suspicion that he was by no means indifferent to Becky, and was therefore doubly reassured.

'I like him,' she announced sunnily. 'He's always nice to me.'

'You,' pointed out her sister, 'don't work for him. Nor, when you last met, had you seriously embarrassed him by gatecrashing his office without scrip or scrippage to identify you. You may find him not quite so keen the next time you meet.'

Chloe, nerving herself to meet her sister's level grey eyes, blushed guiltily and began to bluster. 'I'm sure you're making a fuss about nothing. You never used to be

6

like this. After all, there's no harm done! I'm not a spy and both you and Mr Townsend know it.' She surveyed her sister unflatteringly. 'You've changed.'

It was true. Composed, immaculate, with her unruly curls swept elegantly on top of her head, Becky was almost a stranger. Chloe frowned.

Perceiving this, Becky resisted the temptation to tease further. Abandoning the attempt to keep a straight face, she chuckled.

At once Chloe grinned in relief. 'You're a beast,' she said without rancour. 'You haven't changed, then—why did you go all pompous?'

'I couldn't resist it, I'm sorry,' said Becky generously. 'You looked so thoroughly guilty. Have a drink and forgive me.' She produced a bottle of wine from the lower drawer in her desk, together with two glasses.

Chloe fortified herself with a long draught. 'That's better!'

'Now—as I assume your primary purpose in coming here was not to torpedo my career—you'd better tell me all about it.'

'Er—well,' said Chloe, 'it's complicated.'

'I'll bear that in mind. Say on.'

'And I don't know that you'll be able actually to *do* anything . . .'

'Chloe, stop blethering. What's it all about?'

Chloe licked her lips. 'Mother,' she said succinctly.

'*Mother?*' Becky's eyebrows flew up in pure surprise. 'What about Mother?'

Chloe had recourse to her wine glass again. Then, 'She's broke,' she said sharply.

There was a long silence, and Becky passed a hand over her eyes. 'Broke? But she can't be,' she said blankly.

'She is,' insisted Chloe, 'well and truly. She says she'll have to sell the house.'

Becky flinched. 'But she can't!'

'Well, I don't see that she can do anything else,' said Chloe honestly.

'What on earth has she been doing? Punting recklessly at the vicar's bingo binges?'

'Don't laugh,' said Chloe sharply. 'It's serious.'

'How can it be? I know the trust fund's not large, but it's adequate, and she owns the house. If she hasn't taken to gambling or playing the market I don't see what can possibly have gone wrong.'

Chloe took a deep breath. 'Well, you see, it was Aunt Edith's idea . . .'

Her sister's eyes narrowed. 'Ah yes,' she said, 'Aunt Edith. That well-known freshwater shark. I should have guessed. Tell me about Aunt Edith.'

'She—er—she had this idea. She wanted to start a donkey sanctuary, and she persuaded Mother to go in with her.'

There was a stunned silence. Becky opened her mouth to speak, found she had nothing to say, and closed it again. Chloe watched her anxiously.

'Donkeys,' she said at last, faintly. She thought about it. 'It's no good. It's so impossible, it must be true. What happened to Aunt Edith? Did she sell out of Gilts or something? Did her stockbroker advise her to go into donkeys?'

'You aren't taking this seriously,' Chloe complained.

'I'm trying,' her sister assured her. 'I'm trying my hardest. I just can't—quite—envisage Mother and Aunt Edith in partnership in a donkey farm.'

'Sanctuary,' corrected Chloe automatically.

'*Sanctuary?* You mean it was non-profitmaking?' said Becky gropingly. 'No dividends for Aunt Edith? Has she suddenly become an animal-lover?'

8

Chloe giggled. 'Well, that's what she said at first,' she admitted.

Becky looked at her keenly. 'Why?'

'Because she wanted Mother to help, I suppose. And she wanted somebody else to put up half the capital.'

'*What?*'

Chloe shifted uncomfortably. 'Aunt Edith said they could set up a charitable trust and save lots of money on income tax, and buy Hunter's Meadow and just turn the donkeys out to grass.'

'Hunter's Meadow,' said Becky thoughtfully, 'which just happens to back on to Aunt Edith's property. What happened, Chloe? Was the Parish Council going to run pigs on it or something?'

Chloe looked at her in some dudgeon. 'You have a nasty suspicious mind.'

'I know. It's a remarkable asset,' said Becky tranquilly. 'What was going to happen to Hunter's Meadow?'

'Well, apparently someone was going to develop it, build three or four blocks of flats and a service road. Mother didn't hear about it until they'd bought the meadow.'

'But of course Aunt Edith did. And of course four blocks of flats would spoil her view somewhat. Why didn't she buy it on her own?'

'She said she couldn't afford it,' answered Chloe.

There was a pregnant pause. 'And Mother thought she could?' murmured Becky.

'Well, she's very tender-hearted and she likes donkeys. She'd seen some gruesome programme on television about how people mistreat them and she wanted to do something about it. Since I moved out she's been at a bit of a loose end. People are very kind, but she hasn't got anything to do. I didn't think a donkey sanctuary was a bad idea.'

9

'That,' said Becky drily, 'does not surprise me at all.'

She surveyed her younger sister, reflecting with some surprise how like their mother she was. They had the same speedwell blue eyes, the same air of hopeful innocence, the same grace, the same devastating helplessness. She sighed.

'I suppose you didn't even try to dissuade her?'

Chloe looked reproachful. 'It was what she wanted to do, and I didn't see why she shouldn't do what she liked. After all, she'd never made a fuss about anything we wanted to do when we were younger.'

'And you felt it only fair to reciprocate?' Becky laughed unwillingly. 'Well, that's only reasonable, I suppose. So what's happened now?'

'She—er—borrowed the money. To put into the sanctuary, I mean. And then she found that the RSPCA wouldn't let them do what Aunt Edith suggested and said they had to put up sheds and engage a farrier, and Aunt Edith wouldn't give her any money towards it, so she took everything out of the bank and ...' Chloe ran out of breath.

Becky was looking grim. 'And?'

'And she had to get some more.'

'Who on earth, in his right mind, would lend money to Mother to put up donkey stables?'

'Edward Mallory.'

Becky's feet, which had been resting negligently on the windowsill, came down with a crash. 'Oh no! Oh no, not Edward. He's as big a shark as Aunt Edith. Bigger,' she said impressively.

'He's always been very fond of Mother,' said Chloe weakly.

'He's not the sort of man who does business with people he's fond of. There must have been a reason. I know—I bet he was the developer who wanted to buy

Hunter's Meadow. When the donkey farm goes bust he'll step in and mop up the dregs.'

'He'll mop them up sooner than that,' said Chloe desperately. 'You don't know the worst. Mother borrowed thousands from him. And then he went and got angina and had to go to Switzerland and handed all his affairs over to Charles, and someone has sent Mother a rude letter demanding she pay some huge sum in interest by the end of the month, and she'll have to sell Orchard House and ...'

'Try breathing occasionally,' advised her sister, replenishing her wine glass helpfully. 'And stop flapping. Good heavens, the Mallorys are neighbours. They can't make Mother sell the house. Things can't possibly be as bad as you make out,' she finished bracingly.

Chloe refused to be braced. 'Yes, they can. You don't know how much she owes him.'

'Then you'd better tell me,' said Becky calmly.

She did. There was an extended silence while Chloe stared at her sister, torn between a certain feeling of triumph and despair. Becky had gone white with shock and her hands moved agitatedly.

At last she managed, 'She *will* have to sell the house. We could never muster that much between us. And are you telling me that Charles Mallory has the gall—the sheer indefensible greed—to dun Mother for a sum like that?'

'Well, I suppose it is his money, in a manner of speaking,' said Chloe charitably.

Becky waved that aside, lighting one of her infrequent cigarettes with hands that shook slightly. 'Nonsense, it's his father's. And even if it were his, there'd be no justification for throwing Mother out of hearth and home to get it back. He can make quite enough himself to keep himself in positive decadence—he doesn't need Mother's life-savings as well.'

'We-ell,' said Chloe, now approaching the heart of her mission with delicacy and some caution, 'it is possible that he doesn't personally know anything about it. I mean, Edward must have a lot of odd debts to be collected one way and another, and there's no reason why Charles shouldn't have delegated it all to someone else.'

'Very possibly,' snapped Becky, still seething. 'It would be like him to pass on the task of oppressing the innocent to his minions.'

Chloe sent her a reproachful look but forbore to remonstrate. 'The letter Mother had about the money was signed by somebody called Smart,' she volunteered.

'Oh?'

'We thought it might be a secretary or someone like that. Someone who wouldn't know that Mother was a personal friend of Edward's.'

'Or who wouldn't have cared if he did know,' Becky said caustically.

Chloe regarded her fingernails absorbedly. 'Charles would care,' she remarked. 'Don't you think?'

'He ought to, certainly, but whether he actually would or not is another matter. You never can tell with Charles. I suppose Mother hasn't tried to contact him?'

'She said she couldn't face it.'

'I know what she means. He's a smooth devil. At least with old Edward you know where you are—he may want his profit, but he doesn't go backwards to get it. Perhaps he isn't all that scrupulous, but he isn't—devious—like Charles.'

'You're being unkind,' said Chloe. Here was a train of thought, it seemed to her, which had to be stopped if Becky was to be persuaded to confront the awesome Mr Mallory.

Discussing Mrs Summerson's tangled affairs with her solicitor, Chloe had come to the conclusion that the most pressing problem was to come to terms with her creditor. James Lord had shown little enthusiasm for the task. It was one thing, he pointed out to his innocent client, to know what should be done. It was quite another to propound an extension of a loan amounting to downright charity to a man with as few soft corners and as ready a tongue as Charles Mallory. James, a modest country solicitor for whom Becky had worked when she was at home, saw comparatively little of the Mallorys either socially or professionally. Such barristers as he briefed were seldom concerned with commercial law, but even so he was familiar with the reputation of the magnificent, malevolent Mallory whose few appearances in Court drew as many spectators as Wimbledon.

Chloe, who had suffered from his tongue throughout her childhood, had agreed wholeheartedly, and it had been a unanimous decision to elect Becky as her mother's spokesman. As Chloe said, Becky had always been able to stand up to Charles. Mrs Summerson dissolved into tears and Aunt Edith had been known to gobble with rage whenever his blistering phrases had been turned against them. Only Becky did not. She was undoubtedly the best person to approach him on the delicate matter. The only difficulty lay in persuading Becky of her fitness for the task.

Therefore Chloe assumed her most injured air and said, 'I don't see why you have to be so unkind about Charles. After all, nowadays we don't know anything about him. We haven't seen him for years.'

'I have,' said Becky, clearly brooding rancorously on a previous confrontation.

'Oh, social occasions,' Chloe sniffed. 'Nobody's at their

best on social occasions, even you aren't! You can't judge him by that.'

'I'm not judging him at all,' said Becky with patent untruth. 'He's nothing to do with me, thank God. Though there was a time, as you should well remember, when he was in and out of Orchard House like a yo-yo on a peculiarly short string. And even then he was abominable.'

It was undeniable, and Chloe bit her lip. 'He may have changed,' she essayed at last.

Becky snorted. 'Changed? Charles? Well, he may have shed a few skins, snakes do, I believe. But they get glossier ones in their place. Don't let your charity carry you away.'

'He can be very amusing,' said Chloe indomitably. It was a lie; Charles Mallory had never amused her. The nearest she had ever come to pleasure in his company was when he ignored her, and she was grateful that he forbore to tease. But Becky, she knew, had relished the inevitable exchange of insults, at least on those occasions when Mr Mallory had not come off wholly victorious.

'Yes,' Becky allowed fairmindedly. 'Yes, he can be. He can also be unprincipled and vicious. No, no, Chloe, Charles Mallory is only bearable a long way on the other side of a gin glass about once a year. More than that is distinctly poisonous.'

'He's always very polite,' objected Chloe, at her last gasp.

'He's as bad as his father has ever been,' stated Becky roundly, 'only with a Cambridge gloss on it. Don't deceive yourself, he's dangerous.'

There was a pause. Then, 'It seems a shame,' ventured Chloe, trying another tack. 'I mean, when he first went up to university he used to be terribly attractive. I used to have all sorts of fantasies about him coming home and carrying me away with him. He was super.'

'He's super now, if you like the type. Tall, dark and handsome with a tongue like a sub-machine gun. I wouldn't tangle with him myself, but I'm sure there are plenty of women who do. In fact,' Becky added reflectively, 'I know there are, because I worked with one of his rejects not so long ago and she was very bitter on the subject. He seems to be irresistible if you like bullies.'

'Which you don't,' supplied Chloe resignedly.

Becky gave her that sudden mischievous grin with which she always demolished her own wilder flights of bombast. 'Probably because I'm too much of a bully myself,' she acknowledged. 'Besides, I've known him a long time.'

'And disliked him a long time,' observed Chloe glumly.

'You may be right,' admitted Becky. 'I was a child of strong prejudices and he roused all of them. Even at—what was he then, seventeen? eighteen?—he was an arrogant pig. And stop looking so reproachful! If you hadn't decided to be so damned saintly all of a sudden, you'd come off your pedestal and admit you agree with me.'

'Yes, oh yes, I do,' confessed Chloe cravenly. James, she reflected, would not be pleased. 'He used to terrify me. Well, he still does. I'm not at all surprised you're scared of him.'

Becky sat up very straight. 'I am not,' she stated with great precision, 'scared of anyone.'

Chloe said nothing.

'I am not,' insisted her vainglorious sister.

'You mean, if you were Mother, you'd go and beard Charles in his den?'

'Certainly.'

'Without a qualm?'

'He's human,' said Becky disdainfully. 'Just.'

'And you wouldn't want anyone to do it for you, or come with you or anything?'

'Naturally not!'

'Oh!' Chloe, no mean strategist, crossed her legs and allowed a slight sceptical smile just to touch the corners of her mouth.

Her sister bristled. 'And what do you mean by that?'

'By what?'

'By sitting there looking smug and doubting every word I say. Surely you can't believe that I would really be afraid of Charles Mallory? A man I've known since I was eight?'

'Well, I've known him since I was three and he terrifies me,' pointed out Chloe. 'And what's more, he does the same to Mother.'

'Mother is much too easily impressed,' said Becky loftily.

'Well, she's in a very nervous state at the moment, and you could hardly blame her. She really needs someone to take things out of her hands. Of course the ideal thing,' said Chloe as if suddenly inspired, 'would be for you to talk to Charles.'

She met Becky's burning look guilelessly.

'As you're not afraid of him,' she explained.

Having effectively talked herself into a task for which, Becky was honest enough to admit, she had little relish, she decided to go about it as quickly as possible. Accordingly she sought an interview with John Townsend as soon as her secretary had escorted Chloe to the first floor snack bar to fortify herself after the journey.

Townsend, who had spent no small interval in placating the offended security officials who had complained at length about the English disregard for authority, was not surprised to see her. He stood up as she came into his office.

'Hello, my dear. How is the culprit?'

'Covered in shame,' said Becky, not entirely truthfully.

16

He smiled ruefully, a slow, greying man who never quite achieved the placidity that nature had intended for his large frame. Now his habitually worried expression had sharpened to anxiety during his dialogue with the gatekeepers. As always, however, he calmed himself in Becky's soothing presence.

'The shame I doubt,' he murmured. 'I'm afraid she doesn't realise ...'

'Not for a moment,' agreed Becky peacefully. 'Does it matter? She won't do it again.'

He shuddered. 'I hope not!'

'She wouldn't have done it this time if it hadn't been for a slight crisis at home. I'm afraid I'm going to have to ask for some leave, John.'

He smiled at that. 'Well, you've plenty left and you're entitled to it. When do you want to go?'

'Now,' she said briefly.

'*Now?* You mean today?'

'I mean at this moment. As soon as Chloe has finished her coffee. I'll have to pack and catch the first available flight home.'

'I—see.' He picked up an exquisitely pointed pencil on his desk and began to turn it round and round in his fingers. 'Now.' He sighed. 'You know Becky, your ability to act on these lightning decisions of yours makes me feel very old.'

She laughed. 'No, why should they?'

'Oh, I don't know. It seems such a youthful thing to do, somehow. A call for help—I assume that is the crisis, by the way? someone wants help?—and you down tools and off. I admire that.'

'I can see that it's very inconvenient for you,' acknowledged Becky, suspecting sarcasm, 'but I don't have much choice.'

'I see,' he said again. 'Am I allowed to ask what is the crisis?'

She made a helpless gesture. 'John, I——'

'I know,' he said with thinly veiled bitterness. 'You don't want to talk about it. You don't give your friends much of a chance, do you, Becky?'

'I don't know why you should say that.'

'No, you don't, do you? Becky my dear, you know how fond of you I am. All I want to do is to help, if I can.'

'That's very kind of you,' she began uncomfortably.

'But it's none of my business? Oh, very well, Becky, if that's the way you want it.' He pulled a leave form towards him and said briskly, 'How long do you want? I mean, can we expect you back in the foreseeable future?'

'I don't know,' murmured Becky. 'I'd better take a couple of weeks at least, and I'll write and tell you if I need any more. It shouldn't take long once I've tracked somebody down. There's someone I have to see,' she explained, 'and he can be very elusive.'

'An old friend?' he asked, doodling.

'You could put it like that, I suppose.' Becky was amused.

'*The* old friend?'

She looked at him, startled. 'What do you mean by that?'

'I mean,' he said with barely suppressed anger, 'the one who comes between you and every other man in the universe. The one you won't talk about. The one you pretend not to remember and refuse to forget. *That* old friend.'

Becky bit her lip. 'I don't know who told you,' she said at last, quietly, 'or whether you guessed, but it's not really important. Except that you're wrong about one thing. It isn't the man I can't forget, so much as the gigantic fool I made of myself. That's what sticks.'

'You were close?' he asked gently.

Becky sighed. 'I thought so,' she said sadly. 'Anyway, it's all over and I don't care to be reminded nowadays.'

'I'm sorry,' he said, stiffening, 'I don't want to intrude.' He bent his head and quickly signed the form, pushing it across the desk towards her. 'You'd better fill in the details yourself. Go when you like, of course.'

Her eyes gleamed with self-mockery. 'Before I lose my nerve,' she agreed. And left him wondering exactly what heroic task she had undertaken.

Becky was given an early opportunity to put her courage to the test. Returning to Almcote, much to the un-suspicious gratification of her mother, she came face to face with Charles on Saturday morning. She was backing the large hired car out of Orchard House's awkward corner garage, and at the third attempt she became aware of an audience.

Charles, having clearly given up hope of being able to pass the corner for some time, had stopped his own powerful car and got out and was now leaning on its gleaming bonnet, watching her manoeuvres with a critical eye. She stopped and lowered her window as he strolled across.

Characteristically, his first words were not a greeting. 'We drive on the left in this country,' he informed her kindly. 'Odd of us, eccentric even. But when in Rome, my dear Becky . . .' He held the door open for her. 'Come on. Are you going out or coming in?'

'Out,' she said.

'Very well. I'll do it.'

'How chivalrous,' she mocked, scrambling out of the driving seat.

'Not at all. Otherwise I shall obviously be here all day while you make ninety-nine-point turns. Do you suppose that if I park outside the gate facing in the right direction you'll manage to stay on the left-hand side of the road?'

'I will make the attempt,' said Becky crushingly.

Charles sighed, quite uncrushed. 'Then God help everyone else.'

He started the engine and performed the delicate operation with odious competence.

'Thank you,' said Becky between her teeth.

'Not at all.' He got out and looked down at her for a moment as she stood fighting with her temper. 'Same old Becky!' He flicked her chin with an avuncular forefinger and ushered her back into her car. 'This place has been very uneventful without you, or so I gather,' he remarked. 'I'm not often here.'

'I can imagine,' said Becky with awful sarcasm.

He laughed suddenly. 'I'm sure you can, but don't. You and your sister have always imagined me to be a monster of depravity, and it's time you grew out of it. In fact,' he put his head on one side, 'it's time you were taught some manners.'

'By you?' enquired Becky dangerously.

He chuckled. 'I can't see anyone else taking on the job, can you? You have claws, my child, but you don't intimidate me. To begin with, you can say thank you nicely to me for rescuing a damsel in distress.'

'Entirely for your own convenience,' she pointed out. 'But thank you.'

'*Not* very gracious,' he murmured. 'To make amends you'd better come to the party my stepmother is giving tonight.'

She raised her eyebrows. 'As a penance? You're not very complimentary to Judith's party.'

'Oh, I've no doubt it will be excruciating,' he said, preparing to leave. 'Judith's got one of her women's rights oddities coming—too boring. I rely on you to entertain me.'

And he shot away as Becky, temporarily abandoning her intention of going shopping, went indoors to tell her mother what had transpired.

Mrs Summerson was, not unnaturally, thrown into confusion.

'Oh dear,' she said, adding unconvincingly, 'I mean how nice. But *Charles* ... I'm afraid there's something that I haven't told you ...'

Becky took pity on her. 'If it's about the money you owe the Mallorys, I know,' she said gently. 'Chloe told me.'

'Oh, do you?' said Mrs Summerson, taking the news with unexpected equilibrium. 'But do you suppose that Charles does?'

'We shall have to see. I'll try to find out tonight. So I think perhaps you'd better prime me with the facts.'

Mrs Summerson, rather reluctantly, produced the relevant papers and hung about Becky like an indecisive moth while she perused them.

'What are you going to wear?' she demanded, trying to bring her daughter's mind back to the things that really matter.

'Oh, something long, I suppose. I've got a silk dress in my case that will do.'

'Are you sure? You could borrow something of Chloe's if you liked. She wouldn't mind, and she's left most of her pretty dresses here.'

Becky tore herself away from the papers she was studying and regarded her mother ironically. 'It's hardly going to matter how I look.'

'It always matters how a woman looks,' objected her mother. 'Especially when she has something not very nice to discuss.'

Becky caught sight of her reflection in the study mirror and wrinkled her nose at it. 'I don't actually think that batting my eyelashes at a man like Charles will get me anywhere, but I suppose I can try.'

Mrs Summerson nodded enthusiastically; she was an old-fashioned tactician. 'You can borrow my French perfume if you like.'

Becky laughed at that, but she made a little grimace of distaste as well. 'We're a scheming pair,' she observed. 'I'd feel rather ashamed of myself if it wasn't for the fact that I'm quite sure Charles won't notice.'

But in that she was wrong.

She arrived late to find a sizeable and very smart party in full swing. Rather desperately she wondered how, in such a press of people unknown to her, she was going to find Charles. In the end he solved the problem for her, appearing as if by magic at her elbow.

'Hello, Becky,' he said mildly enough, though there was a distinct gleam of amusement in his eyes. He lit her cigarette for her courteously and let his gaze wander over her dress. 'Dazzling the natives?'

She sniffed. 'I don't know what you mean,' she said in a cool tone.

His thick eyebrows rose. 'Don't you?' he said, apparently astonished. He made a sweeping gesture, 'Your face, your hair, your air—French perfume, French clothes ...'

'I live in France,' she reminded him gently, aware that she was blushing and furious that she should.

'Paris?' he murmured, taking her arm and steering her to a vacant window seat.

'No. Why?'

'To the experienced eye,' he said loftily, 'that dress screams Paris.'

She was amused in spite of herself. 'And your eye is experienced,' she commented.

'I pay Judith's dress bills,' he explained blandly, 'and I occasionally get to see what I'm paying for. Am I wrong?'

'No, you're not wrong, though I'm amazed you should notice.'

'On any other woman, I probably wouldn't,' he said surprisingly. He took her lightly by the shoulders and held her away from him assessingly. 'They told me you'd changed,' he was thoughtful. 'I couldn't imagine it. Now I see what they mean.'

'I wish I could think that was a compliment,' said Becky uneasily.

'Why do you think it isn't? Don't your friends and relations like what you've done to yourself? Or aren't you accustomed to compliments?'

'Not from you,' she pointed out.

'True enough. But then I'm a simple sort of fellow, I just say what I think.'

She looked at him ironically. 'You mean your insults aren't calculated? You're just nasty by nature?'

He laughed. 'You haven't changed that much. That's the authentic Becky speaking.'

'*Oh*,' she was conscience-stricken. 'And I meant to be civil to you tonight,' she said unguardedly.

His eyes widened in innocent amazement. 'You overwhelm me,' he said dulcetly. 'What have I done to deserve such marks of favour?'

'You haven't done anything,' Becky acknowledged ruefully. 'It's rather what we've done that's the trouble.' She squared her shoulders and looked at him candidly. 'I'm afraid we—er—haven't behaved very well. Could we talk somewhere? Privately, I mean?'

His eyes had narrowed. 'We could hardly be more

private than we are here. I take it, when you say "we" you're referring to your mother?'

She swallowed. 'Yes.' She found she couldn't sustain his regard, and dropped her eyes to her glass.

There was a pause.

Then Charles said slowly, 'I see. She's told you about her escapade. I wondered if she would.'

'She didn't think you knew,' muttered Becky, not looking at him. 'It was a business affair. We thought somebody junior was dealing with it.'

'Annabella Smart wouldn't thank you for calling her junior,' he replied in a preoccupied tone. 'As a matter of fact I've only just found out. Raven Enterprises was one of my father's less savoury activities, and I'm about to kill it. That was why I've been looking at the books. Otherwise I'd probably only have bothered with the half-yearly balance sheet as he did last year, and then I wouldn't have found out. That's why I'm here really—I thought I'd better see your mother myself.'

Becky flinched. 'Oh no! Oh, please don't. She's so upset, you mustn't. Look, Charles, I'll do everything I can; I'll arrange something, truly I will. But you mustn't disturb my mother.'

In the silence that followed she dared only one swift glance at him before swinging round to look out of the darkened window. His eyebrows were contracted above the bridge of his nose, which gave him a satanic aspect. She could feel the anger in him and trembled.

At last he said, 'You really haven't changed at all, have you? Still leaping to conclusions, still throwing yourself into the breach. You're wasted on this age, you know. You should have been a knight in shining armour.'

'Promise me you won't go and see her,' she insisted.

Unexpectedly he gave in. 'Very well, if that's what you want. I gather she had appointed you her agent—

you'd better come and see me tomorrow. Obviously I can't talk business here. Besides, we shall be eating soon, when all the local flotsam leave.' His tone was suddenly impatient. 'God knows why Judith's asked them all. It's not as if they're even friends of hers. Look, there are the Lords, looking as if they can't wait to get away.'

Becky took a small sip of her gin and said, 'Perhaps they're tired. Friday isn't always the best day for a party, if your guests have been at work all week. I expect James wants to get home to put his feet up.'

'James Lord being one of the workers of the world, eh?'

She lowered her eyes and sipped again. One thing about Charles, she reflected, he was always acute.

'And so am I, come to that,' he added, 'so you can stop looking so sanctimonious.'

She looked up at that, outraged. 'I wasn't!'

'No?'

'No.'

'Becky my child, you're a poor dissembler. You were standing there despising all poor Judith's guests for their lack of activity. They are butterflies, you said to yourself, lilies of the field, while I am virtuous, honest, sober and industrious!'

She showed her teeth in what a casual observer might have mistaken for a smile. 'Damn you, Charles!'

He smiled down at her very sweetly. 'Come, come. I thought you were going to be civil to me tonight.'

'Oh, yes, I was,' she gasped, conscience-stricken. 'But you always rub me up the wrong way.'

'You don't,' he said judicially, 'take much rubbing.'

'Oh, now that's not fair. You were outrageously rude, and all because I said poor James was probably tired.'

He laughed. 'Simple jealousy,' he explained. 'I also am very tired and I'm not getting any sympathy for it, *And* I shall be up to the small hours talking to this rabble, I don't doubt.' He looked down morosely at his glass and swirled the amber liquid in it a couple of times before tossing it off. Then he took her glass. 'What are you drinking? Let me top it up.'

'It could do with some ice,' she admitted, 'but no more gin, please. It gives me a headache.'

Charles looked round the room with dislike. 'This whole set-up gives me a headache.' He took her hand and half-dragged her through the crowd to where the bar stood by the open french windows. It was a damp night and the air was full of the smell of rain and azaleas. Becky breathed it in thankfully.

'Damn it, there's no more ice. It's just melted into a puddle.'

'Oh, it doesn't matter,' she assured him, only to have her words received with a wry grin.

'You don't have to be *that* civil. Nobody wants a slice of lemon that's been pot-roasted in gin. We'll go into the library; there's a tray in there. If nobody's disturbed it, there's usually some ice.' He scowled at a velvet smoking jacket that showed every sign of edging between them and eased it, none too gently, out of the way. 'We'll go round the back through the garden. Come on.'

Becky followed perforce.

Outside it was spitting with rain, but Charles showed no remorse for exposing her to the elements. Indeed, he didn't so much as inquire after her wellbeing.

All he said was, 'You'll have to run. It's raining.'

And so she found herself pelting along the damp stone terrace in his wake, her elegant skirts bunched unceremoniously in one hand to keep them from the ground. He flung open the doors into the library, helped her across the frame, and snapped on a reading lamp on the desk.

Becky put hands to her dishevelled hair. 'Oh, I'm

thoroughly rumpled!' she complained, torn between indignation and amusement.

'Are you?' he said absently, investigating a tray of decanters.

She glared at his back. 'Charles Mallory, you're a thoroughly inconsiderate man,' she announced.

He turned at that, with an air of a magician, and wafted a glass under her nose. 'Inconsiderate? When, braving the night air and troops of invading hedgehogs, I have ploughed across enemy country to get you a civilised drink?'

She accepted it, inclining her head graciously. 'There is that, of course. Perhaps I forgive you.'

'Thank you.' He poured his own drink and sat down opposite her in a large and comfortable armchair. It was also, she observed in some surprise, distinctly shabby. He waved a cordial hand at a similar chair on the other side of the empty hearth. 'Do sit down. Now you're here, you might as well get your breath back before you start insulting me again.'

She resisted the impulse to reply in kind, and sat.

'Well!' He regarded her over the top of his glass with an expression that she found unreadable.

Now she had the leisure to observe him properly, she discovered that he looked tired, and more than tired. In the last few months since she had seen him he had lost weight and now he looked haggard. When he was talking his eyes lent him animation, but when, as now, he was lost in his thoughts he seemed almost skeletal in his immobility. Concerned, she observed the deep clefts in his cheeks which seemed to have been driven across his face by pain, or something like it, which must have been nearly unbearable.

She said, very gently, 'I was so sorry to hear about your father. Is he any better?'

At once the brooding eyes left whatever inward landscape they were contemplating and lit with laughter.

'Time for conversation?' he drawled. 'What are we going to talk about? Our respective parents? Cabbages and kings?'

'Charles,' she said dangerously, 'are you calling my mother a cabbage?'

He looked startled and then his mouth twitched in comprehension. 'It never occurred to me that you might think of my father as a king,' he said. 'I didn't really want to talk about either of them tonight. Can't we leave business until tomorrow? I'd like at least to *pretend* that this is a pleasant party.'

'I wasn't thinking of business, merely of Edward's health,' she returned stiffly.

He sighed. 'In that case, I apologise. He's well enough, or I suppose he is. I took him over there and saw him installed. They say he has to have complete rest and quiet.'

'Good heavens,' said Becky with simple horror. 'Poor old Edward.'

He gave her a bleak little smile. 'As you say. It'll probably kill him.' He swallowed his whisky in the quick, nervous movement she had noticed before and went to pour another. With his back to her he said, 'But what's the alternative? If he stays here, Judith drags him along with her on her social round, or else he decamps to London and starts wheeling and dealing, just as he's always done. So it's Switzerland or an early grave. Though I'm not sure he doesn't regard the nursing home as just about the equivalent.'

Becky watched him helplessly. 'I'm sorry,' she said.

He had picked up the decanter and held it for a moment, aimlessly, almost as if he were surprised to find it in his hand. 'Yes. Well. At least he's alive, which after the pace at which he's been taking the last year is more than he deserves.'

'How long will he have to stay there?'

'Switzerland?' Charles sounded a long way away from her again. 'God knows. Until his heart improves, I suppose. Or his family becomes less of a trial. Or he signs away all his business interests and reconciles himself to twiddling his thumbs for the rest of his life. Or all three. How can I tell?' He shifted his shoulders impatiently, as if ridding himself of something that clung. 'It's kind of you to be concerned, but the truth is that nobody knows, including the doctors as far as I can see.' The suspended decanter was allowed to tip further and he splashed a generous tot into his glass.

Bringing it back to the hearth, he lowered himself on to the rug at her feet and sat with his back propped against the stout legs of her chair. Becky had the feeling that he had done it deliberately; it hid all expression from her. Looking down at him, she marvelled at the finely sculpted profile, the deeply shadowed lashes, as long as a woman's, the crisp hair. Certainly, she thought, almost surprised at her discovery, he was quite as attractive as he had ever been. Age—and what was he now? thirty-seven? thirty-eight?—had only added distinction. And even at graceless eighteen he had been the sort of boy to charm the most hardened feminist. Sharply, she remembered him soothing her redoubtable Aunt Edith until that lady had made quite a favourite of him. She sighed.

Charles turned his head at that, and looked at her thoughtfully. 'Tired?'

'No.'

'No? Bored, then?'

'Not that either,' she denied.

'Well, you can't be drunk on warm gin. So it must be— what? Nostalgia? Unrequited love? Hunger?'

She laughed. 'Perhaps a little of all of them,' she admitted, and he put up those fine brows of his.

'Expound!' he commanded.

'I was just thinking of how good you used to be at chatting up Aunt Edith,' she confessed.

'I still am,' he said smugly. 'That accounts for the nostalgia. What about unrequited love?'

She looked down at his bright face, turning the glass round and round by its stem, and Charles observed this sign of inward agitation interestedly. It was the only thing that gave her away. At last she said gently, 'That's my business, I think.'

He frowned quickly. 'Oh, of course. And the hunger is presumably accounted for by the fact that it's now nearly ten o'clock and Judith still hasn't summoned us to the trough. Shall I go and complain?'

Becky shuddered at the thought. 'No, please don't. I'll withstand the pangs as best I may.'

He sprang up and collected a glass dish of salted nuts from the tray of decanters and bottles. 'Have a peanut,' he said chivalrously.

She did.

'So what have you been doing since last I saw you? Brussels, wasn't it? You were holding Townsend's hand at the conference. Really, that man is a total incompetent. When are they going to kick him out and give you his job?'

'Never. If it comes to that, he's more likely to take over mine.'

'Oh? Moving on?'

She sighed again, a little drearily. 'I don't know, I suppose so. I've been there long enough, and soon I shall begin to get bored. Besides, I don't want to live in France all my life, and if I don't decant myself soon, I shall never summon up the energy. My contract runs out next month. I shan't renew.'

'What'll you do? Come back here?'

'I can't imagine it.'

He frowned. 'Why not?'

She shrugged helplessly. 'It wouldn't work. I've changed, Charles, even though you may not be able to see it; I've changed a lot during the last two years, and some of the changing has been—painful. I don't hold the same beliefs any more; I've changed my priorities.'

'So?'

'Well, my mother hasn't,' she explained. 'There's a lot she believes in, and automatically assumes that I believe in, that has just—gone. I can't explain it any other way. If I came back here to live with her, my mother would find out how different I've become from her image of me.'

'You always were,' he said coolly.

That startled her. 'What?'

'Your mother was never very bright about you.'

Somewhere in the distance a gong began to sound and he urged her, still protesting, to her feet.

'Come along, or it'll all be gone, and I'm hungry.'

'But you can't just leave it like that,' she spluttered.

'What? Oh, your mother's image of you. What a silly girl you are! For years she's gone around telling people what a sensible, straightforward girl you are. *Sensible!*' he snorted, opening the door for her into the dining room.

In silent outrage, Becky swept past him.

By now the party had shrunk, or been whittled down by its accomplished hostess, to a mere dozen persons. A sumptuous buffet was set out on a table in one corner of the room and Becky made her way towards it, conscious that more than one pair of eyes had observed and speculated upon her appearance from the library with Charles.

She lifted her chin and helped herself to soused herring, a dish she detested.

Soon enough she found James Lord by her side. He was an old, uncritical friend and she smiled at him.

'Hello, Becky my dear, I hoped I'd be able to have a a word with you. It's good to see you back. I'd have come over sooner, but either you were being monopolised by young Charles or I was fighting for my life with that girl he's talking to now.' The jerk of his head in the direction of a striking-looking woman was less than complimentary.

Becky surveyed the lady critically. 'Doesn't look his usual style,' she observed, 'too tatty.'

He hooted with laughter. 'For the lord's sake don't let her hear you say that! She's a tub-thumper. Women have more in their lives than making themselves beautiful for the predatory male.'

'Oh.' Becky was nonplussed. She cast a doubtful look at the lady under discussion, deep in animated conversation with Charles who was looking just a little amused. 'Is that what she's been saying to you, James?'

He nodded. 'Over and over again. Loudly. I couldn't get rid of her. She's French,' he added gloomily, 'very voluble, the French.'

Becky began to laugh. 'Oh dear! But less than ever Charles' type, I would have thought. He likes his women to be a good audience, but they're not expected to take the floor themselves.'

'Oh, as to that, I gather she's a friend of Judith's.'

'You amaze me,' said Becky with truth, surveying their hostess shimmering in a voluminous gold kaftan. 'Judith been converted to the Cause?'

James Lord looked uncomfortable. 'She *is* rather anti-men at the moment, since Edward was sent off to

Switzerland. Charles has rather a tight hand on the purse-strings, I surmise.'

'Very probably,' agreed Becky. 'He wouldn't miss an opportunity to tyrannise.' She paused thoughtfully. 'Do you mean that Judith has imposed this apostle of women's liberation to berate Charles? What an extraordinary idea! She can only annoy him.'

'Yes, perhaps. You and I may realise that, but Judith isn't a very bright——' he broke off. 'Oh, lord, they're coming this way!'

It was too late to retreat as Charles, with wicked innocence, gracefully introduced his companion to them. 'This is Véronique Marin,' he murmured. 'Becky Summerson, James Lord.'

'We have met,' said Véronique, nodding briskly at James. He shrank, and she looked at Becky keenly. 'I have wanted to meet you, Miss Summerson. Charles tells me you are One of Us.'

There was a startled pause, then Becky said carefully, 'I'm not quite sure in what sense you mean, Miss Marin.'

'I mean you live your own life. You have your work. You are free.' She glared at James, who was staring at Becky with undisguised horror. 'Oh, I don't know the English. You are a—what is the word, please?'

'Career person?' offered James.

Charles choked. Miss Marin, conscious that her audience was not altogether with her, was most creditably prepared not to take offence.

'Ah well, you are very silly,' she said tolerantly. 'You do not know how important the work is.'

'What work?' ventured Becky, perceiving Charles to be incapable of speech.

Véronique beamed upon her. 'I'm an activist,' she informed her. 'I am here for a conference on women's rights. Soon there will be no need for conferences.'

'I don't,' mused Becky, 'see that there's exactly a need for them now.'

'Not?' Véronique was shocked. 'But, Miss Summerson, you and I may be free, but thousands of our sisters are not.' She made a large gesture which would be very impressive on a hall platform. 'Every year, more and more of them sell themselves into slavery . . .'

'Eh?' jerked out James, simple amazement causing him to forget his prudent resolve to take no further part in any conversation which included Mademoiselle Marin.

She looked at him innocently. 'Marriage,' she interpreted.

'Oh. Oh, I see.' He subsided, rumbling like a hardly roused volcano.

'Why,' she said, warming to her theme, 'in some places—and I'm talking about Western Europe, not the Sahara—girls aren't even allowed to choose their own husbands. It is a terrible . . .'

She continued at length, and James rolled an anguished eye at Becky. That lady was beginning to find Mademoiselle Marin a distinct annoyance. She wanted her to go away so that she could talk to James; or failing that, she wished she would simply fall silent. It was extremely wearing to be addressed as if one were a public meeting. She began to count to ten under her breath. When she had finished, as Mademoiselle Marin very clearly hadn't, she decided the time had come to interrupt that erudite monologue.

'Anyway,' she remarked in a clear little voice, 'I don't think arranged marriages are such a bad idea.'

Miss Marin had actually moved on from arranged marriages to the iniquities of the university selection system, but she was quite prepared to take up cudgels on the former field. The only thing that seemed to trouble her was the identity of her opponent.

'You, a woman, say this?' she demanded burningly.

'I do,' snapped Becky.

James cast her a look of mingled respect and gratitude. Charles stopped laughing, one eyebrow shooting up in incredulity.

'Marriage,' said Becky largely, 'is a job of work, like any other. It's only a success if you work at it properly.'

'And how would you go about that?' murmured Charles. His expression was one of polite interest, but Becky knew him well enough to detect the laughter in his voice, however prim he tried to sound.

She lifted her chin. 'It's like any office—one would have to be prepared to compromise.'

'You mean,' Véronique groped for words, '*you* would marry like this? Not some poor little ignorant peasant girl, but *you*. Would you marry a man your father or your brother chose for you?'

She caught Charles' sardonic eye. 'Yes,' she said defiantly.

'Brother and father has she none,' he remarked idly, 'you can't put her to the test.'

Becky glared at him, and one corner of his mouth went up in a smile that was oddly rueful.

'Let me understand you,' he said patiently. 'Are you really saying you'd marry someone—anyone—as a matter of convenience? Without any reservations? No let him be handsome, let him be rich?'

'Certainly.'

'Not even some mutual affection?'

'I've told you—I regard marriage as a career like any other, and you can't stipulate what sort of colleagues you'd like. One would hope to be reasonably compatible, of course.'

'And if you weren't?' asked Charles curiously.

Becky shrugged. 'A condition of work to which one

would accustom oneself. I've worked for some stinkers in my time, but one gets used to it in the end, I find.'

'Easy enough to say,' he commented.

Becky ground her teeth. 'Are you trying to provoke me, Charles?'

'To be honest? Certainly.'

'I am honest!' She almost stamped her foot.

'In thinking that marriage is just another commercial contract?'

'Yes.'

He held her under a long, maddening regard before shaking his head sceptically. Becky danced with fury, then she gave a false tinkling laugh and remarked to the room at large, 'Charles can never bring himself to believe that I'm not as silly as he likes to think me. He finds it so trying that I have a mind of my own.'

Charles, in the act of lighting a cigarette, stopped, an arrested expression on his face. Then, very deliberately, he put the flame to the cigarette, inhaled deeply and stowed the lighter away in his pocket.

Only when all this had been completed to his satisfaction did he say, 'Very well, marriage is a job. You, I think, will shortly be out of a job, and need a new one. Marry me.'

CHAPTER TWO

In retrospect Becky was willing to concede that she had allowed herself to be carried away. In fact, her irritation with the eloquent Miss Marin was such that she had been drawn, all unthinking, into the avowal which had provoked Charles to issue his challenge. That it was a challenge and no more, she had no doubt—and of course, once having taken her stand, she was not going to back down and give him the satisfaction of crowing over her.

Nevertheless, by the time she sought her bed that night she was bitterly regretting her tenacity. Of course, it had been worth it at the time. She dwelled pleasurably on the memory of Charles' face, utterly disconcerted by her answer. Yet by three o'clock, as she still lay anxious and sleepless in the bed she had occupied since she was eight, she reproached herself furiously. Really, she had no more self-control than when she was a child! She had allowed Charles to infuriate her, just as he had always done, and inevitably her tongue ran away with her. And once it had done so, she was too proud to retreat.

At first she had been so taken aback, she had stared at him with her mouth open.

James had said furiously, 'Good heavens, my dear, he must be out of his mind!'

'To contemplate marrying Becky?' Charles had drawled. 'You're probably right, but hardly complimentary.'

Becky's lips had twitched, but James had been really angry.

'What nonsense is this?'

'No nonsense,' said Becky, disliking the ironic glint in Charles' eye. 'It's perfectly straightforward, James. I want a job. Charles wants a wife.'

'Positively made for each other, you see,' explained her antagonist dulcetly.

Becky cast him a look of dislike. 'It would be a marriage of convenience, of course; I think they're often the best kind, don't you?'

Ignoring the rider, James said seriously, 'But what about your family, my dear? What about your mother? I'm sure she wouldn't approve of this.'

'Ah, but Becky has outgrown her mother's old-fashioned prejudices, haven't you, my love?' demanded Charles wickedly. 'We were just talking about it before dinner.'

Under James' austere look of surprise, Becky found herself blushing. It did not sweeten her temper or soften her feelings for Charles.

'That was *not* what I meant,' she said with restraint, by now thoroughly roused, 'and of course the marriage wouldn't be nearly so convenient if my mother were to dislike you.'

She paused as if debating with herself. Charles gave a soft, triumphant laugh.

'Running for cover, Becky?'

His tone of light contempt would have infuriated a saint, she thought, and after an evening of his baiting, her mood was far from saintly.

'But there again,' she said, as if she had not heard him, 'I *will* need another job, and I haven't actually got another offer in hand.'

He stiffened, shocked, and she hoped, alarmed.

'I will marry you,' she said sweetly.

For a moment there was a little silence that she suddenly felt might be dangerous. Charles' eyes narrowed and she thought she saw a flash of anger, quickly suppressed.

He recovered himself quickly. 'Do we sign a contract or simply have a gentleman's agreement?'

'You may trust my word,' said Becky, flown with gin and bravado.

'And I have witnesses.'

The witnesses for their several reasons were looking quite disgusted with the little comedy. James made an inarticulate noise indicative of protest and Charles smiled at him.

'It's all right, James, I'll take her home now, she shan't embarrass you any more. Say goodnight,' he instructed her as if she were a six-year-old, 'and come along.'

Becky allowed herself to be swept through the door.

'Do you have a coat?' asked Charles.

'No. I drove over.'

'Oh? I'll send the car back tomorrow, then. I'm going to drive you home.'

'That's not necessary,' she replied stiffly.

'Oh, but it is. We've got a lot to talk about.'

'I don't see what!'

'Well, we've got to set a day for the wedding, for a start,' he said cheerfully.

She was appalled at this prosaic observation. He saw it and laughed softly.

'Unless you propose to jilt me already?'

She stiffened her spine. 'Certainly not!'

'No, it wouldn't look good, would it?' he agreed blandly, ushering her out of the front door. 'Not after such a very impassioned defence. Here we are.' He opened the door of a dark car standing in the drive.

Becky got in gracefully. She found she had nothing to say.

He closed the door and then joined her. He didn't start

39

the car at once but sat peering at her in the half-dark.

'I wasn't joking, you know. We really have got things to talk about.'

He was rattled, she thought, and she hugged herself pleasurably.

'Running for cover, Charles?' she taunted.

Suddenly he laughed. 'You're a hussy, my child! It's time someone took you in hand.'

'I thought you were going to,' she said innocently.

'I am. I most certainly am.'

'We'll see,' she observed. 'What did you want to talk to me about?'

He ignored the implicit challenge. 'Me,' he said succinctly.

'I beg your pardon?'

'Me. My side of the bargain—what I want out of this convenient marriage of ours.'

'Oh,' she was bewildered. 'Yes, of course . . .'

'First,' he said, turning the key in the ignition and allowing the car to roll gently down the drive to the main gates, 'I want you to get rid of Judith.'

'*What?*'

He chuckled. 'That could have been better phrased; I don't mean I want you to murder her or anything extreme like that.'

'I'm relieved,' said Becky drily.

'No, no, if murder were the answer I could have done it myself, with pleasure. What I want you to do is to dislodge her from the house in London.'

'Your house in London?'

'Since my father made it over to me, yes. It became mine when he went to Switzerland.'

'If it belongs to you, why haven't you dislodged her yourself?'

'I lack the resolution,' he assured her.

'I find that difficult to imagine,' she rejoined.

'Especially as I'm also my half-sister's guardian. I can hardly turn Tessa out of my house, but I don't want her mother. I rely on you. Get rid of her.'

'That seems a little hard,' said Becky judicially. 'After all, it must have been Judith's home for some time.'

'She's never lived there until this year, she's always said that it's much too inconvenient and put up at an hotel. It's only a little house. No room,' explained Charles carefully, 'for large parties. Anyway, Judith doesn't like London; she prefers New York or Paris. She's only moved in this year to be awkward. And I want her out.'

'But not Tessa? I've got to expel Judith and keep Tessa?'

'If you wouldn't mind.'

'I don't *mind*,' said Becky, 'I'm just not sure whether I can do it.'

'I'm sure you're more than a match for Judith.' He sounded as if he were smiling. 'And Tessa seems quite a good kid. I'd like her to live with us.'

Becky was surprised. 'Certainly,' she said, not quite managing to banish it from her voice.

He looked sideways quickly. 'You *do* mind.'

'Of course not. I'm just a little—disconcerted—to find you caring about a tiresome teenager,' said Becky, recalling with rancour an insult from the past.

Charles laughed. 'You really do think I'm armour-plated, don't you?'

'Are you telling me you've mellowed?' she said scornfully. 'When Chloe and I were Tessa's present age, I remember you being distinctly acid on the subject of teenagers.'

'Tessa,' he said calmly, 'is not such a disaster as you and Chloe were. She even seems quite sensible sometimes.'

41

'Oh.' Recalling Mrs Summerson's account of the behaviour of Miss Mallory, Becky digested this with a large pinch of salt. 'So: one Tessa, no Judith. Anything else?'

'What a very good wife you mean to be,' he murmured. 'Nothing else at the moment.' He had drawn up outside Orchard House. He regarded her curiously. 'You really *do* mean to work at it, don't you?'

'Of course,' she said coldly, refusing to rise to the mockery in his voice.

'And it's going to take a good deal of resolution, hmm?'

'You needn't worry,' she retorted, 'I don't give up easily. And I've never walked out on a job yet.'

She put her hand on the door handle, but he stopped her, quite gently.

'Splendid,' he said, bending his head to kiss her.

Her first instinct, a triumph for him and source of complete dismay to Becky, was to slap the confident smile from his face. But in a second she had herself in hand.

At last he drew back thoughtfully, stroking his long supple fingers along the line of her jaw.

'Yes, well.' He looked unforgivably amused. Holding her by the chin, he turned her face towards the light of a distant street lamp and scrutinised it. 'That's going to need a little attention,' he murmured.

Stiff with outrage, Becky said between her teeth, 'I'll bear it in mind.'

Charles laughed aloud at that. 'I'm sure you will,' he agreed ambiguously.

He had left her then, not even waiting until she was safe inside the house before pulling away with considerable acceleration. Becky had stood for a moment in the damp lane, glaring after his disappearing lights in some dudgeon. As always, she felt, Charles had come off rather the better in their encounter. And with masterly tactics he had left her to break the news to her mother on her own.

Not entirely unexpectedly, Mrs Summerson was waiting up for her daughter. Becky paused momentarily outside the sitting room whence a faint light under the door advertised her mother's continued presence long after her usual bedtime, then she squared her shoulders and walked in, only to stop short in surprise.

While she was prepared for her mother she had not expected her sister, whose visits to Orchard House were necessarily infrequent.

'Hullo, Chloe,' she said, divesting herself of her coat, 'come to hold our hands?'

'I telephoned her,' explained Mrs Summerson agitatedly. 'I thought we'd better have a family conference.'

'A what?' gasped Becky, briefly forgetting that her family were as yet unaware of her rash commitment. 'What on earth ...? Oh, about the money, I suppose.'

'What else?' demanded Chloe, regarding her flushed cheeks narrowly. 'Mother rang me up and said that you'd been to see Charles. What did he say?'

'Er—about the money?' parried Becky feebly, feverishly trying to determine how much of Mr Mallory's words could safely be retailed to her auditors. She was fairly sure that they would be out of sympathy with most of the sentiments he had expressed that evening and equally sure that, edit his remarks as she might, they would eventually be regaled with the whole interchange. The whole thing, she was beginning to realise in dismay, had been just too public.

Mrs Summerson did not try to disguise her amazement. 'Well, of course about the money. What else?'

'What indeed?' responded Becky with a giggle that her mother thought singularly foolish.

'Well?' Chloe was impatient.

'Well—er—we didn't really talk about it,' Becky admitted weakly.

There was a disbelieving silence.

'Then—you—didn't talk about it,' Chloe repeated. She exchanged a bewildered look with her mother. 'Why? Wasn't Charles at the party after all?'

'Oh yes.'

'Surrounded by other people?' Chloe went on gropingly. 'Otherwise occupied? Impossible to get on his own?'

'No, not exactly.'

'So you *did* talk to him.'

'Er—yes.'

'Then, in heaven's name, if not about the money, then what?'

Becky smiled reminiscently. 'Cabbages and kings,' she shrugged.

'*What?*'

Mrs Summerson felt it was time she took a hand in the unequal dialogue.

'Sit down, Becky,' she said sharply with an authority no less effective for being long unused.

Becky did.

'Now,' she went on, 'stop grinning to yourself and tell us what happened.'

'Oh, nothing really,' Becky said airily. 'You know what these parties are. Nobody talks to anyone for very long ...' She met her mother's eyes, and they stared at one another for a second before Becky flushed and looked away. With an effort she went on, 'Charles was—was much in demand. We had to talk—er—very quickly ...'

Mrs Summerson was not deceived. 'Becky,' she said with foreboding, 'what have you done?'

There was a pause. Then Becky, kneading her hands

together in a trick she always had when agitated, said defiantly, 'I got engaged to him.'

'You——' Chloe was lost for words. 'Engaged?'

'You agreed to marry him?' demanded Mrs Summerson, who liked to have things clear.

'Yes.' Becky sounded distinctly sulky.

'Married?' moaned her mother, sinking on to the couch.

'To *Charles*!' added Chloe, following suit. She glared at Becky. 'You're not safe to be let out on your own, do you know that?'

'It—seemed a good idea at the time,' Becky appealed.

'You must be out of your mind,' her sister told her roundly, 'and for that matter so must he. You dislike him only one degree less than I do. You can't marry him! It's unthinkable, I can't imagine why he asked you in the first place.'

'He asked me,' said Becky wearily, 'because I'd made him so mad he thought he'd call my bluff. I always had the unhappy knack of rousing his temper. So *I* called *his*.'

'What?'

'I wanted to talk to him about Mother's affairs. I really,' she said ruefully, '*did* try. Only somehow it annoyed him, and he started baiting me. And then he introduced me to some dreary female who thought I was a freedom fighter for women's rights.'

'So?' said Chloe, lost.

'Well, she said how terrible it was that women were still slaves in the twentieth century. It was,' said Becky with disdain, 'immeasurably tedious. She went on and on and on, and was rude to poor James Lord: and Charles just stood there laughing. So in the end she came to arranged marriages. I'd just about had enough, so I said that I thought arranged marriages weren't a bad idea. I was perhaps,' she allowed reflectively, 'a little pompous on the subject. Anyway, I got up Charles' nose, and he said if I was so keen on a marriage of convenience I could marry him. So I said I would.' She dwelled on the memory with satisfaction.

There was a wail from her mother. 'Becky, how could you? It's so unlike you to be . . .' she was lost for a word.

Chloe, however, was not. 'Outrageous,' she supplied grimly. 'And it's not in the least unlike her, Mother. She's always been willing to go to any lengths to get the better of Charles. But I never thought you'd go so far as to *marry* the man, just to gain your point.'

Becky had the grace to blush.

'It's so unladylike,' moaned her mother. 'What must people have thought?'

'Much the same as you do,' said Becky wryly, 'that we were both mad.'

'He can't have meant it,' said Mrs Summerson hopefully. 'It was one of his nasty jokes.'

'It was,' agreed her elder daughter.

Mrs Summerson sighed with relief. 'Well, that's all right, then. He'll come round and apologise in the morning.'

Chloe looked at her mother in some exasperation. 'Oh no, he won't.'

'Yes, he will. He always used to as a boy when he and Becky had a fight. He was always the first to make it up. Say what you like about Charles,' said Mrs Summerson fairmindedly, 'he doesn't bear grudges.'

'Nor, presumably,' said Chloe with irony, 'does he back out of engagements. Think for a moment, Mother. Becky has publicly accepted him. Whatever reasons he might have had for asking her in the first place, he can hardly suddenly announce that he's changed his mind. It would be frightfully insulting.'

Mrs Summerson was much struck. 'I hadn't thought of that.'

'No, and obviously neither had Becky. If she had, she might have kept quiet and let Charles take the game for once. As it is—well, what are you going to do, Becky? Marry him out of sheer perversity?'

'That doesn't sound very nice,' protested her sister.

'Well, it isn't very nice, is it? Marriage,' pronounced Chloe, who had successfully avoided it for some years, 'is a serious business, not to be flung into in a fit of pique.'

'I can't help thinking,' ventured Mrs Summerson, 'that you've been—well, not very *kind* to Charles, perhaps.'

'Kind!' snorted her daughter. 'Is he kind to me? No, no, Mother, I've been rash, I admit it, and I haven't behaved very well, but it was at least as much Charles' fault as mine.'

Mrs Summerson frowned. 'I wish I could be sure of that,' she sighed. She seemed to reach a painful conclusion and fixed her younger daughter with a compelling eye. 'I think tea would be a good idea, Chloe. Would you mind putting the kettle on, there's a dear.'

Chloe, looking from the mother's look of gentle determination to Becky's mulish expression, acquiesced ruefully.

As the door closed behind her, Mrs Summerson possessed herself of Becky's hand and said, 'You aren't doing this because of all that money I owe him, are you?'

Becky's frown vanished and she laughed. 'Don't be feudal, Mama, of course I'm not. I wasn't even thinking about money. I was just in a temper.'

'Ah,' Mrs Summerson meditated profoundly. 'I would be very sad,' she pronounced, 'to think that any daughter of mine accepted a proposal of marriage because she was in a *temper*.'

Becky's frown returned blackly, but Mrs Summerson

47

ignored it. 'You'll have to apologise to him, of course. You can't possibly go through with it.'

'But . . .'

'You don't love him,' said Mrs Summerson with finality. 'Or do you?' she added innocently.

'Good lord, no! Do you have to ask?'

'I thought not. Well, one day you'll meet someone you do love, and then you'll be very thankful that this ridiculous situation didn't get out of hand. You'll have to speak to Charles tomorrow.'

'Oh, Mother!' said Becky despairingly. As her mother bristled she went on hastily, 'Yes, yes, I promise. I'll speak to Charles. I'll positively grovel, if that will make you feel any happier.'

'It's you who'll feel better,' Mrs Summerson assured her.

Becky chuckled. 'Because it leaves the field open for Prince Charming when he finally gallops over the horizon?'

Her mother flushed. 'You can laugh if you like, but you'll be glad one day when you fall in love properly.'

'I've been in love properly, Mother,' Becky reminded her gently, 'and it was a complete disaster.'

'Yes, but *next* time . . .'

Becky shook her head. 'No next time, Mother. I'm not going through that again.'

Mrs Summerson looked distressed. 'You can't judge all men by Tony Boyd.'

Becky blenched. 'Mother . . .' she protested.

'Oh, I know you don't want to talk about it, and I've respected that up to now. But you can't condemn all men because Tony Boyd was so—so——' She paused, lost for a suitable adjective.

'Human,' supplied Becky. 'That's all he was, Mother, just human. Fallible and a bit weak. The fault was all on my side; I built him up into a hero. Only I've grown up a bit since then, and I now know that storybook heroes don't step out of the pages of fairy tales.'

'You'll find someone, one day,' repeated her mother indomitably. 'Someone kind and reliable and amusing and——'

'Wholly mythical.' Becky shook her head. 'Men like that went out with the gryphon and the unicorn,' she said with affectionate mockery. 'It's a wholly fabulous beast. Face it, Mother.'

Mrs Summerson bit a lip. 'Once you wouldn't have talked like that.'

'I told you, Mama, I've grown up and grown wise. Well——' she corrected herself wryly, 'wiser. I'm not looking for a crock of gold any more.'

'Don't talk like that,' said Mrs Summerson sharply. 'Anyone would think you were a hundred. It's silly and I don't like it, any more than I like your behaviour this evening. I don't know what you think you're about, Becky, but I don't find it very nice. It's not the way I brought you up.' She gathered up her handbag and bed-time reading with great dignity. 'I don't want to talk about it any more. What you and Charles decide to do is entirely your own affair, but I shall think very poorly of you if you hold him to his word when you don't even pretend to love him.'

She swept out.

Becky dropped her head despairingly in her hands for a moment before crossing to the window and staring out into the dark. It was true that she didn't love Charles, but he must know that. Her mouth twisted. The whole of Almcote was perfectly well aware of the disastrous course of her only love affair! For the first time in two years she allowed herself to think about Tony Boyd.

He had been her aunt's farm manager, fresh from New

Zealand, full of zeal for his job and with an infectious enthusiasm for rural life. Becky, who by that time had spent four years in a country solicitor's office and was beginning to feel jaded, was quite enchanted with him. He had zest and enterprise and an energy that swept her along with him. Within a month of his arrival she had acknowledged to herself that she was in love with him, within six months they were engaged.

It had become apparent at once that Aunt Edith did not like him as a prospective husband for Becky, however much she might value his services as a farm manager. That had rankled with Tony. The one flaw in Becky's happiness was the way Tony would rant about Aunt Edith's meanness and snobbery. After all, she would point out, Aunt Edith was an old lady with different values from their own. What did her approval or otherwise matter to them? But of course it mattered a great deal in the end.

For when an opportunity had presented itself to get rid of Tony Boyd, Aunt Edith had taken it with both hands, and had succeeded.

Becky shut her eyes, remembering all too vividly the humiliating interview at which Aunt Edith had accused Tony of theft. He had blustered to begin with, but in the end he had admitted it. Aunt Edith had been triumphant: Becky, shocked, was nevertheless still deep in love. She could understand that to Tony, without friends, family or resources of his own except what he earned in a strange country, the temptation to acquire one or two of the valuable things that Aunt Edith left scattered about her house must have been almost irresistible.

'You have no right to judge him,' she had told her aunt coldly.

'If I haven't, who has? I'm the one he stole from,' the old lady replied testily.

50

'For precisely that reason,' Becky's legal mind had answered. 'You're not impartial. You can't be accuser and judge.'

'You'd rather I called in the police?'

'Of course not!'

'Well, make up your mind,' Aunt Edith had snapped. 'It's your choice.'

Becky had not understood her. Hurt and disappointed as she was by Tony's behaviour, she didn't perceive the use to which Aunt Edith intended to put her discovery. Tony, however, had a better appreciation of Miss Summerson's Machiavellian methods.

'What do you want us to do?' he demanded tersely.

'Oh, nothing, nothing. It's entirely up to you. If you want to stay here and marry Becky, then I shall have no choice but to tell the police. You might be a dangerous criminal for all I know.'

'You mean you won't prosecute Tony if he leaves Almcote?' said Becky slowly.

'No.'

'But you said ...'

'I won't prosecute your young man,' said Aunt Edith with careful emphasis, 'if you break this ridiculous engagement of yours.'

'I won't do it,' said Becky instantly. 'That's blackmail.'

'Sue me,' retorted her aunt, unimpressed. 'Well?'

'I don't see that there's anything else we can do,' Tony had said at last, half apologetically. 'Look, Becky love, I'm sorry ...'

But even then she had not understood.

'I won't do it,' she had assured him blithely. 'We'll go away, get married. Aunt Edith won't press charges—she'd have difficulty in proving them anyway.'

'Oh, would I?' had said that lady, laughing malevolently. 'Well, would I, young man?'

'No,' he had admitted reluctantly, 'no, she wouldn't. Becky, for God's sake don't stir up any more trouble. I'm in enough as it is.'

'I told him,' Aunt Edith explained in passing to her stunned great-niece, 'that you only inherited this farm, as he seemed to think you would, if I approved of your husband. I'm certainly not leaving it to this good-for-nothing.'

Appalled, Becky had found nothing to say. She had stared dumbly at Tony Boyd.

'It's true,' he agreed at length.

'I don't care,' she had said, in a last-ditch stand for their freedom. 'I don't care what she does with her rotten old farm. I'll be all right with you.'

But he hadn't quite bargained for that. 'Ah, I couldn't make you give up your inheritance,' he had said nobly, just fractionally too late for it to sound spontaneous. In fact, it was a decided spur-of-the-moment excuse, and made Aunt Edith cackle with laughter; even Becky, who was in love with him, could not credit his sudden disinterested chivalry. 'I couldn't ask you to leave everything, your family, your friends, the life you've always known.'

In love she might be, but Becky was by no means stupid and she found his melodramatics offensive. 'Are you about to tell me you can offer me none of the comforts to which I'm accustomed?' she had demanded dangerously.

'Well, can I?' He had spread his hands helplessly.

'Don't be silly, gel,' Aunt Edith interrupted, 'the boy doesn't want to go to prison, even if you'd be happy to let him. Give him his ring back and be sensible.'

Becky had looked only at Tony. 'Is that what you want?'

He mumbled and shifted in embarrassment, but it

was soon enough apparent that Aunt Edith was right. She had put the ring down on the table between them and walked to the door without speaking.

'Don't be silly,' called out Aunt Edith. 'Best thing that could have happened all round. You'll get over it.'

'Oh, be quiet,' Tony had muttered, moved at last by Becky's pale face. 'Look, Becky, don't you see ...'

She had swung round on them then, shaking with anger.

'You disgust me,' she said clearly. And, as he flinched, she added, 'Both of you.'

Within two hours she had packed her bags and left Orchard House and Almcote, and though she had returned from time to time for brief weekends to see her mother, she had never visited Aunt Edith. And she had never, until today, contemplated returning to it permanently.

The door opened to admit Chloe bearing a tray, and Becky swung round sharply.

'Did I startle you? I'm sorry. I thought tea rather a weak idea, so I've brewed some hot chocolate. I hope that's all right.'

With an effort Becky came back to the present. 'Oh yes, perfectly. Mother doesn't want any, though; she's gone to bed.'

'I know,' said Chloe, putting the tray down, 'she came into the kitchen to tell me.' She gave her sister a steaming mug, regarding her frowningly. 'What are you trying to do, Becky? Even if you want to marry Charles Mallory, telling Mother comfortable lies about being past the age of a grand passion is no way to go about it.'

In spite of herself, Becky choked with laughter. 'I don't recall saying precisely that,' she demurred.

'Oh? Well, that's what Mother told me.'

'I merely tried to point out that Charles and I knew

53

each other well enough for long enough not to expect high romance.'

'And Mother took offence?'

'Not quite. Although yes, I suppose she did in a way.'

'Of course she did. You've transgressed every one of her rules tonight, you know. You've behaved badly, you've done it in public, and you've caused people to talk about you. And you have repudiated the sacred name of Love,' concluded Chloe dramatically, striking a pose.

Becky choked on her chocolate. 'You're a donkey!'

'No, I'm not,' said Chloe cheerfully, collapsing on to the hearthrug. 'It's perfectly true.' She observed with satisfaction that the drawn look had gone from Becky's eyes. She had been a little frightened when she first came back into the room to perceive how sternly Becky was staring out of the window. 'I've had the same lecture from her on many an occasion as I suppose you've just had. Did she call you a cynic and tell you to wait for the right man?' she added with a certain professional nonchalance.

Now Becky was really laughing. 'Don't be mischievous.'

'So she did. I could have told you she would when she sent me out of the room—I suppose she didn't trust me as a wholly sympathetic audience.'

'You mean you might have undermined her effect?'

'I could have tried,' Chloe was tranquil. 'Poor Mother, she's very sweet.'

'I don't see that she need have worried,' observed Becky. 'You've struck me as very harmonious on the subject. Positively unanimous.'

'What, about you not marrying Charles? Ah yes, there we're united, but for different reasons. Mother wants you to fall in love and marry someone fantastic. She cherished hopes of John Townsend for years.'

'Good heavens,' said Becky in real amazement, 'but I work for him!'

'Mama, unlike you or me, does not see that as an insuperable obstacle. Never having worked for anybody herself,' mused Chloe, 'I suppose she's never realised how well one gets to know them. *Much* too well to marry them.'

'Or to be asked to do so,' pointed out Becky. 'John Townsend wouldn't have me as a gift.'

'Probably not,' agreed Chloe with a grin, 'but you can't expect Mother to believe that.'

'All right, probably she wouldn't. So what have you got against me marrying Charles?'

Chloe frowned into the fire. Then, 'Charles,' she said briefly.

'I beg your pardon?' Becky was startled.

'It's not because I dislike him, or anything like that,' Chloe assured her, 'or at least, not very much. Though I admit he scares me a bit sometimes.'

'Well, he doesn't scare me.'

'No, I know. That's——' Chloe hesitated. 'I think that's what. worries me when I think of you marrying him. You're not *enough* scared of him. You don't seem to have any sense of self-preservation where he's concerned. You just go sailing in blithely without thinking.'

'I certainly did tonight,' agreed Becky ruefully.

'Yes, you did. And anyone who knows you would have expected you to do exactly what you did, given the circumstances. Charles himself must have foreseen it. In fact, I wouldn't be surprised if it wasn't all a plot that he'd hatched up to trap you deliberately. It would be like him.'

'Oh, don't be so silly! What could he possibly have to gain by it?' Becky's tone was sharper than she had intended because of her sneaking and growing suspicion that her sister might have some grounds for her assertion.

55

'Lord, how should I know? I can't fathom Charles' thought processes. But if—suppose for just one minute that my idea is possible—*if* he wanted to marry you, there was no other way that he would ever have got you to agree than by making a challenge of it. Now was there?'

Becky shivered. 'Don't!'

'Was there?'

'I don't know. Perhaps not. But why should he bother?'

Chloe shrugged. 'I've told you, I can't guess. Perhaps he needs a wife for his income tax. Or perhaps his father wants a cosy daughter-in-law to come home to. You always got on well with Edward.'

'Tessa,' explained Becky.

'I beg your pardon?'

'He wants somebody to dislodge Judith and take over Tessa.'

'Well, there you are, then. That solves it.'

'No, it doesn't,' snapped Becky. 'Why me?'

'Because he knew you were reliable and he knew you wouldn't interfere with him,' said Chloe fluently. 'He didn't have to pretend to be in love with you.'

'No,' Becky's tone was a mite forlorn. 'No, he certainly didn't have to do that.'

'So—problem solved. And you fell into the trap as neat as you please. Really, the man's positively diabolical! You're no match for him.'

'What an awful pun!' objected Becky, almost absent-mindedly. 'I think you overrate his ingenuity—and my desirability, even as a guardian angel for Tess. There must be plenty of other people much easier to persuade to take it on. Good heavens, he could pay a governess, for that matter. He doesn't have to get *married*.'

'It does seem a bit drastic,' agreed Chloe, disappointed, 'but mark my words, you'll find that he had some other reason. It was all thought out. You won't persuade me that it wasn't. People like Charles don't do things on the spur of the moment.'

By the time she got to bed Becky found that, as had occasionally happened to her before when she was over-tired, she could not sleep. The shadowy shapes of child-hood furniture, long forgotten and now suddenly re-visited, filled her mind. She found herself remembering idly; incidents from the past crowded into her brain leaving no room for consideration of her most urgent problem. She tossed and turned impatiently, but she found she could neither concentrate on the immediate issue nor fall asleep properly.

Some time before dawn she did finally manage to make up her mind that she must confront Charles. It was quite ridiculous to imagine that she could marry him. It was not simply that her mother and Chloe were op-posed to the idea—no, she assured herself, she was per-fectly capable of standing up to them when she was sure she was right. But this time not only was she not sure of herself, but a good many of their objections found an echo in her own wavering mind.

Of course, there was no question that Charles had be-haved abominably and thoroughly deserved a taste of his own medicine, but that was no real excuse for her to behave equally badly. If she was honest, she had to admit she could not contemplate anything as serious as marriage for no better reasons than those she had given Charles. In spite of his faults she had been totally com-mitted to Tony Boyd; if she married Charles she would be merely using him. She found herself wincing in the dark at her own cynicism. No, even Charles did not deserve to be treated so badly.

She sat up, biting a thumbnail distractedly. Marriage was clearly out of the question. She had told her mother she was not going to allow herself to fall in love again, and it was no exaggeration. For two years she had guarded her heart very successfully. Yet, if she wasn't prepared to discard her vigilance, she wasn't entitled to marry anyone. Certainly not Charles, who was in his way, she suddenly realised, as guarded as herself.

But if she was not to marry Charles what should she do? Becky felt as if, by coming home like this, she had already said goodbye to Strasbourg. As she had told Charles, her job there had ceased to engage her whole attention, but there was more to it too. Despite her disclaimer to Chloe, she was perfectly well aware that John Townsend was rapidly coming to rely on her as more than a congenial colleague. It surprised her that her mother, who had met him only once and that long before Becky herself had begun to suspect the nature of his feeling, should have discovered it. He was a kind, quiet man for whom she had a great affection, but not of the kind which would lead her to marriage. The simplest solution was to leave.

Then what? Becky thumped her pillow like an ancient enemy. Another job in a city, which she hated? A country practice somewhere? But country solicitors were notorious for preferring their junior partners to be male. James Lord might take her back, of course, but could she face the thought of returning to Almcote? She had made the surprising discovery during the course of the discussions downstairs that, while she could not support the thought of returning to Almcote on her own, it was perfectly tolerable if she were married to Charles.

'I suppose that's really why I agreed,' she told herself with loathing, 'because it seemed to be an easy way of coming back home without having everybody speculating wildly. I wanted to use Charles as a shield. I'm despicable; Mother is quite right—I must tell him first thing in the morning.'

But first thing in the morning found her still asleep; in fact she slept heavily till nearly noon. Mrs Summerson judged it best not to disturb her and indeed, when she eventually emerged, urged her to return to bed. Becky was pale and heavy-eyed and looked more than a little feverish.

'You don't look at all well,' said her anxious parent. 'Why don't you lie down? After all, you've done a lot of travelling these last couple of days. It was bound to catch up with you, especially after last night's excitement. I'll bring you some lunch up on a tray.'

'No, no, I'm perfectly all right,' insisted Becky. She gave a wan smile. 'Except for an uneasy conscience. The sooner I confess the better. I'm going to talk to Charles now.'

'A very good idea,' smiled her mother. 'Use the study phone. No one will disturb you.'

However, in two minutes Becky was back again, looking distraught.

'He's not there,' she exclaimed tragically. 'He's gone back to London.'

'Oh, well, I expect you can get hold of him there,' said Mrs Summerson comfortably. 'Come on, Becky, back to bed. You look terrible.'

She did. Which wasn't surprising, since, as subsequently appeared, she had caught gastric 'flu. For five days she stayed in bed, crawling out only at regular intervals to telephone Charles in London: she was wholly unsuccessful. His secretary in chambers assured her that her messages to Mr Mallory were faithfully delivered, but he never managed to return her call. His telephone at home was simply never answered.

At last Becky fought her way through Mrs Summerson's maternal concern and was given a pass up to London to see Charles on the strict understanding that she was to have lunch on the train and to leave before the rush hour.

From Paddington Becky went straight to Charles' chambers. If he were out she was quite determined to stay and wait for him, no matter how long it took.

Perhaps fortunately he appeared to be in. His secretary, after giving her an odd look, installed her in a creaking leather chair while she went to see whether he was free, while another secretary provided her with coffee.

'You don't look very well, if I may say so,' she told her briskly.

Becky restrained a grimace. 'I've had 'flu,' she said baldly.

'Oh, I'm sorry! But I'm glad you're better now. I suppose you'll have a good deal of arranging and shopping to do?'

Becky was blank.

'Ought I not to have said anything? I'm sorry,' said the efficient secretary again, 'but we were all so pleased to hear Mr Mallory's news. I hope you'll be very happy.'

'Er—thank you,' said Becky, looking as if she had been struck.

The secretary thought she must have been very ill indeed, poor thing, and how very inconsiderate it was of Mr Mallory to keep her sitting in the draughty outer office when he had a nice fire in his room.

The next half-hour was a nightmare to Becky. It seemed as if all the world had heard that Charles Mallory's future wife had suddenly popped up like a rabbit out of a magician's hat and came to observe the spectacle. Certainly she met a good many interested people, but their interest was on the whole kindly and did not justify her almost hysterical sensation of being trapped. By the time she had received the good wishes of half his colleagues and all his subordinates she was, with some memory of Chloe's dire warnings ringing in her ears, quite convinced that Charles was sitting somewhere behind the scenes masterminding the whole ghastly parade. When his secretary eventually summoned her to his presence she was more agitated than he had ever seen her, kneading her hands together ceaselessly.

He frowned. 'This is very unexpected, Becky. I thought you were fixed in Almcote.'

'I had to talk to you,' she said with less than her usual composure.

'Oh? More about your mother's tangled affairs?'

'Rather my own tangled affairs,' she returned with a ragged little laugh.

He stood quite still, regarding her watchfully, but his voice was light when he answered her. 'Oh? Are you in debt too?'

'I think perhaps I am,' she said soberly. 'Charles, I haven't behaved very well. Last Saturday—I was in a rage and I let you stampede me into stupidity.'

'Stupidity? You mean when you said you'd marry me? Strange,' he mused, 'I would have said that's one of the few signs of sense I've seen in you in a number of years. However, do I take it you now want to back out?'

Becky bent her head. 'Yes,' she muttered.

He sat down opposite her behind his untidy desk and offered a cigarette across it. 'Mother been getting at you?' he said conversationally. 'I knew she wouldn't like it.'

She accepted thankfully. 'No, she didn't. And she was quite right.'

'I don't agree, but say on.'

She raised her head and stared at him. 'Say what? I've told you, I made a mistake and I'm sorry. But it *was* a mistake and I don't want to compound the felony by going any further. Already everybody here seems to know all about it.'

He was amused. 'Well, what do you expect? It's still a feudal society in chambers, you know. When the young master get himself engaged it only takes one vassal to read it in *The Times* for the news to fly round the place.'

'*The Times!* Oh, no, Charles! You haven't done that!'

His eyes narrowed. 'Naturally. It seemed obvious. I assumed that when you made promises you kept them.' The words bit.

Becky stared at him. He was sitting very straight in his chair, his eyes on her unforgivingly. To her subsequent shame she succumbed, for the first time in her adult life, to ignoble panic.

Dropping her head in her hands, she began to shake.

'I *can't*,' she said desperately. 'Please, Charles, don't make me.'

CHAPTER THREE

For a moment Charles said nothing. Becky cast one scared look at him and found his expression unfathomable. He was turning his fountain pen round and round in his fingers, staring into the middle distance.

At last he said slowly, 'I can't make you do anything, and if I could I wouldn't try once you'd made it plain you disliked the idea. There's no need to throw a tantrum.'

Becky sniffed. 'I'm sorry,' she said in a small voice, 'I've been rehearsing what to say all the way up in the train. In the end I didn't do very well, did I?'

'Oh, I don't know,' he said drily, 'you made your point quite effectively.' He came round the corner of the desk and perched on it, swinging one foot negligently. 'What happened?' he asked. 'Run out of steam?'

'Run out of bravado,' she confessed. She blew her nose hard and said with resolution, 'I rather got carried away last Saturday—I wasn't thinking clearly.'

He chuckled. 'I would have said you were thinking very clearly. You took the wind out of my sails all right.'

'I did, didn't I?' she said with unconscious wistfulness, then she gave herself a little shake. 'But I shouldn't have been so hasty,' she censured herself. 'I mean—you and I —it's quite ridiculous.'

Charles raised his eyebrows. 'Are you being rude to me, Becky?' he enquired softly.

'No, of course not,' she said remorsefully. 'Oh dear, I keep saying all the wrong things! I just meant that we know each other too well.'

'Do we?' He was enigmatic. 'Well, if you say so. What do you want to do?'

She stared at him. 'It's obvious, isn't it? Abandon the whole idea, of course.'

'Oh, of course. So you want me to contradict the notice in *The Times*?'

She bit her lip. 'I—I suppose so.'

'And there's my colleagues here. They'll have to know; the sooner the better. We can make a start with them,' pursued Charles.

She flinched. Without appearing to notice it, he nevertheless took due notice of the fact and was encouraged.

'*And* our respective families, though I suppose yours will greet the news with general rejoicing. My father will be very disappointed, however, and so will Tessa. I'd promised her she could spend her summer holidays with us.'

Becky swallowed. 'I—I didn't think of that.'

'Not,' he assured her with wholly spurious chivalry, 'that you must allow any of that to weigh with you. You must do just what you think is right. It may be a little embarrassing to begin with, but the fuss will soon die down when people find something else to talk about.'

Becky was puzzled. 'What fuss? Why should anybody bother? Most of my old friends have probably forgotten about me. After all, I've been away for two years.'

'I, however,' said Charles, 'have not.'

Becky clapped a hand to her mouth in horror. 'Oh, what a *fool* I am! Of course you haven't. Oh, why didn't I think of that?'

'It's not important,' he assured her.

'But it is,' she insisted. 'It would make you look an awful fool, wouldn't it? To get engaged and break it off all in one week.'

He shrugged. 'Possibly.'

'And it's all my fault.'

Charles was amused. 'I wouldn't put it quite like that,

but if it worries you there might be a solution that would end this engagement of ours and salve your conscience at the same time.'

'What solution?' demanded Becky.

He was absorbedly tracing pictures in the dust on his desk and took a little time to answer. When he did he gave the impression of choosing his words carefully.

'Well, you could stay engaged to me—purely as a public relations exercise, you understand—for some token period. Say six months.'

'I don't understand. How would that help?'

'Well, lots of people break these things off after a while, don't they? They get tired of each other, or meet someone else, or just decide that marriage isn't for them after all. It doesn't look quite so—personal, let us say—after a decent interval.'

'I suppose not,' agreed Becky doubtfully. 'If you say so.' She pondered. 'Is that what you want to do?'

'It is,' said Charles, a little tensely, 'entirely your decision.'

'Oh, but that's not fair! I want to do what you want.'

'How very flattering,' he said dryly.

Becky smiled sadly. 'It's not really. I can't help seeing I've got you into a horrible situation, and it's only fair that I do what I can to make up for it.'

His lips twitched. 'Thank you, I appreciate that.'

'So it's settled, then?'

'If that's what you want. You'll give me—shall we say—six months?'

'Yes, if you like. Does it matter?'

Charles smiled at her charmingly. 'Not unless you have other views. I merely thought that six months would give us the summer, and we might be able to take Tessa on holiday after all. If it wouldn't interfere with your own plans, of course.'

Becky was taken aback. When she had agreed to Charles' suggestion she had not envisaged quite so close an association. She had assumed that they would continue to live their present separate lives, remaining merely nominally engaged, and it disturbed her to find Charles had other ideas. He saw it and bit back a smile.

'I still have the same problems,' he reminded her, 'and you could still help me if you would.'

'To look after Tessa?'

'And dislodge Judith. I'd be very grateful.'

Becky looked distressed. 'Oh, but Charles, how can I?'

'I leave that to you, but I'm sure you're quite capable of it. Look, the London house is being redecorated at the moment, so Judith wouldn't descend even if she wanted to, it's much too uncomfortable. You could move in as soon as you leave Strasbourg and make sure the place stayed uncomfortable.'

'Move in?' Becky gasped. 'You must be out of your mind!'

'Why?' He was surprised. 'There's a sort of flat—well, not much more than a glorified bedsitter really—on the top floor, that I used to use when I was qualifying. It's not large, but it has its own entrance and you could at least camp there until you find somewhere of your own to live.'

She was dubious. 'I suppose so.'

'You are still intending to leave Strasbourg?' he asked.

'Yes.'

'So what else are you going to do?'

'Oh, heaven knows! Get a new job, I suppose.'

'In London?'

'I imagine so,' she admitted.

'Well, there you are, then,' he said triumphantly, 'it would be convenient for you and of very great service to me.'

66

'If you put it like that ...' she murmured.

'What are you going to do now? Go back to France?'

'I'll have to, at least to give in my notice.'

'And then what?'

'Oh, about a month and I'll be back. I needn't really work out my notice because I've plenty of leave left—I didn't take a proper holiday last year—but it will take me a month to put my stuff together and ship it back to England.'

He was thoughtful. 'So it sounds as if you need a holiday. That you're due for one, at least.'

'I suppose I am,' said Becky indifferently.

'Ah.'

'What does that mean?'

He gave her a mischievous smile that was more than a little rueful. 'It means I've just had an idea that *I* think excellent, but which I am almost certain won't appeal to you.'

'Try me,' said Becky, amused.

'It's Tessa. She has a rather extensive half-term coming up. She'll have finished her exams and apparently they give exam candidates a fortnight or some such thing because they have to go back to school before term starts. She will probably need a holiday too.'

Becky was suspicious. 'Charles, are you being Machiavellian?'

'If I was, I'd hardly admit it,' he pointed out cheerfully. 'All I'm suggesting is that you come away for a couple of weeks with my sister and me. That'll give you the opportunity to decide whether you can bear to see more—of either of us. And it would be fun for Tess, I hope; she hasn't had a good time this last year.'

She acquiesced suddenly, to his unexpressed surprise. 'Oh, very well. I mean,' she corrected herself conscientiously, 'thank you. Where do you suggest we go? Or have you already got that all worked out?'

'Yes,' he said, ignoring the slight sarcasm, 'I don't like to misuse my holidays. I don't get enough of them to waste.'

'Oh!' Becky tried not to sound dismayed. 'You mean you like to pack all the sightseeing you can into a fortnight?'

Charles shuddered. 'I mean I like to spend the absolute minimum of time doing anything except lying on the beach in the sun. If you and Tessa want to chase Greek temples or climb mountains, that's your affair.'

'I see,' said Becky, relieved. 'I must say that sounds a good deal more civilised than I was expecting.' She stood up.

In Charles' eyes there was a distinct twinkle. 'I *am* a good deal more civilised than you expect,' he told her solemnly.

'You could hardly be less,' she snapped with a momentary return of antagonism, and was instantly ashamed of herself. 'Oh, I'm sorry! I didn't mean it and certainly ought not to have said it when you've been so very forbearing. I really am grateful, Charles.'

She gave him her hand, which he held for a moment, looking at her intently.

'Not at all. The—er—obligation is all mine.' He released her hand and opened the door for her with a quizzical smile. 'Let me know when you leave for France, but leave all the arrangements for the holidays to me. My secretary can deal with all three bookings at the same time.'

'Thank you.' Becky paused in the doorway. 'Charles, about Mother . . .'

'What about your mother?'

'The money——' she began with difficulty, but he broke in, the smile vanishing.

'That's my affair.'

'No, it's not,' she objected, 'and you can't keep refusing to discuss it with me.'

He sighed impatiently, as one goaded beyond endurance. 'All right, come and see me before you go back to France. But don't stew about it, for heaven's sake! It's not worth it.'

'It is to Mother,' she said with dignity. 'But thank you, anyway. Goodbye, Charles.'

'I'll hold your hand as far as the ground floor,' he told her, ushering her attentively through the outer office.

It was a little like going on a Royal Progress, thought Becky, as she bowed graciously to a blur of faces. Charles accepted all the attention quite as his due, she noted with some amusement.

In the courtyard they parted, she pausing only to say, 'May I tell Mother? About our engagement only being a convenient fiction, I mean.'

Charles hesitated. 'Do you want to?'

'Yes. Yes, I think so.'

'Then you must do so.'

She sensed his displeasure and laid a deprecating hand on his arm. 'Only Mother,' she promised, 'no one else, not even Chloe. And I'll swear Mother to secrecy.'

'Presumably it's worth it to reassure her that she won't actually be netting me as a son-in-law. Though it will rather give the game away if she looks too happy.'

Becky laughed at his rueful tone. 'Oh, there's no fear of that,' she assured him, preparing to move away. 'As long as there's the slightest tie between you and me, no matter how tenuous and public, she won't stop worrying.'

Charles grinned, his whole face suddenly young and alive. 'I find that very encouraging,' he said, much to her mystification, and raised a hand in salute as he turned back inside the building.

The journey home was less exhausting than that up to town, presumably, thought Becky wryly, because she now had a comparatively easy conscience. It was with a light step that she walked the half-mile from Almcote station to Orchard House. Her mother, however, was waiting anxiously with all sorts of comforts from freshly brewed tea with muffins to a hot water bottle to revive her daughter after what she was sure must have been a harrowing experience. Perceiving this, Becky laughed and hugged her gratefully.

'There's no need to flap, Mama. I'm feeling positively revived.'

'Was it very difficult? Was Charles nasty to you?' demanded Mrs Summerson, buttering muffins assiduously.

'Charles,' said Becky soberly, 'was a good deal nicer to me than I had any right to expect. And no, it wasn't all that difficult, once I'd got the preliminaries off my chest.'

Mrs Summerson began to spoon a generous helping of last year's apricot jam into a pot. 'So now you're free again?'

'Er—not quite.' Becky switched off the kettle which had begun to boil and made the tea. 'I'll tell you all about it, but let's settle down by the fire first. It's hardly warm outside. I'll take the tray.'

She did so. Her mother, with uncharacteristic reticence, forbore to demand an instant explanation, and it was only after her second muffin that Becky actually told her what had passed.

'And it's a deadly secret,' she concluded, reaching for another muffin and reinforcing its already liberal coating of butter. 'It would make Charles look so silly if it got about.'

'And that matters?'

Becky blushed. 'Of course, as it's mostly my fault in the first place.'

Mrs Summerson pondered. 'That's true, of course. I must say I think Charles has behaved very well.'

'He could hardly sue me for breach of promise,' objected Becky with a buttery giggle.

'Don't be flippant. He could have been extremely unpleasant, and what's more you'd have asked for it. I think you should be grateful to him,' her mother reproved her.

'Oh yes, well, of course I am,' said Becky impatiently, 'but I can't go on treating him as if he's a plaster saint just because he's been generous for once.'

Mrs Summerson's eyes flashed, but she did not retort and after a minute said in a carefully neutral voice, 'Did you manage to discuss the money with him this time?'

Becky gave a little choke of laughter. 'I tried, Mama, really I tried. And he told me to come back next week—or rather before I go back to Strasbourg. I don't think the matter's urgent.'

Mrs Summerson looked injured. 'Oh yes, it is,' she snapped. 'I've had another letter from the R.S.P.C.A. I'm at my wits' end.'

With an effort Becky brought her mind back to the contemplation of her mother's problems.

'Surely we can stall them for the moment?' she said. 'In fact, as the whole enterprise has been so unfortunate, why don't you just sell the land and go back to being a housewife and mother?'

'Because of the donkeys,' said Mrs Summerson reproachfully. 'I couldn't turn them out.'

'But they hardly sound comfortable,' said practical Becky. 'If you've got to put up all these expensive sheds and things, they'd be better off in some sanctuary that's —er—more professionally run.'

Mrs Summerson looked upset. 'I wouldn't like that.'

'Possibly not, but I'm sure the donkeys would. Then you could sell the land, divide the proceeds between you and Aunt Edith, and pay off the loan on this house.'

'But that wouldn't be very fair to Edith. After all, the meadow does back on to her garden.'

'Aunt Edith,' said Becky coldly, 'is quite capable of shifting for herself.'

'I wouldn't be too sure of that. She's an old lady,' said charitable Mrs Summerson, 'and she's getting more and more infirm. I believe she's quite a martyr to that horrid rheumatism.'

Becky, who was now well aware that her aunt's attacks of rheumatism were largely political, snorted.

'It's true,' insisted her mother, 'she hasn't been out of the house since Easter, and then it was only to go to church, and Edward Mallory sent his chauffeur for her. Otherwise she hasn't stirred since Christmas. In fact it would be rather a nice gesture if you went to see her. She must know you're back.'

'No!' said Becky forcefully.

About to protest, Mrs Summerson caught her eye and subsided. It was only to be expected, she supposed sorrowfully; Aunt Edith had been more or less responsible for breaking Becky's first engagement and, while she couldn't regret the termination of the affair, Mrs Summerson did sometimes wonder whether Edith hadn't been a little high-handed in her conduct. Perhaps Becky had good cause for her resentment.

'Well, we won't argue about it,' she said pacifically.

'I suppose,' Becky said in tones of academic enquiry, 'she hasn't offered you any practical help? Like offering to buy out your share in the meadow? Though knowing my grasping Aunt Edith,' she added, 'she would only do that at a knock-down price.'

Mrs Summerson bit her lip. The truth was that the

elder Miss Summerson had indeed offered to buy her share of the land for a sum that was, according to the invaluable Mr Lord, even less than its worth on the market.

'I don't like to hear you talk about your aunt like that,' she said sharply. 'She's—er—she may have got very difficult lately, but she's a great age.'

'No greater than a lot of people who manage to stay reasonably pleasant people,' objected Becky. She found her mother was looking very downcast and patted her hand consolingly. 'Don't worry, we'll sort it all out. It's not your fault.'

Mrs Summerson had recourse to her handkerchief. 'You're so kind to me,' she quavered. 'Everyone's so kind to me, when I've been very silly. Oh, if only Edward were here!'

'It's awkward that he should fall ill at just this juncture,' agreed Becky.

Mrs Summerson looked shocked. 'It's far worse than that—he's very poorly. At first they didn't think he'd live.'

'I'm sorry,' said Becky, startled.

'So I should hope. It's very wrong of you to think of poor Edward's illness as an *inconvenience*. The poor man has had a lot to bear this winter, in fact it makes me ashamed to think of it. Here am I, making a fuss over nothing compared with Edward's troubles.'

'Very philosophical for one on the edge of bankruptcy.'

'Oh, *money*,' said Mrs Summerson disparagingly. 'That's not Edward's problem.'

'Manifestly not. It's yours, however, and if you don't do something about selling Hunter's Meadow you'll end up in a debtors' prison. I do not,' said Becky strongly, 'look forward to the prospect of visiting you in Newgate.'

Mrs Summerson chuckled. 'I'm an awful trial,' she ack-

73

nowledged. 'But it is only money, and no matter what happens, as long as the Trust is intact I shan't be quite destitute. I'm not at the end of my tether like poor Edward.'

'All right,' said Becky resignedly, 'poor Edward is worse off than you are and must be treated with forbearance. I'll buy it. What's happened to poor Edward? Apart from being sent off to some costly and comfortable sanatorium, I mean.'

'Family problems,' said Mrs Summerson darkly. 'It was all too much for him, and he had a heart attack. That's why they packed him off to Switzerland and Charles has come home.'

'Come home?' echoed Becky in amazement. 'Come, come, Mother, you're letting your charity run away with you again. You can't really think he'd quit the fleshpots to put up his boy scout tent in Edward Mallory's backyard. Charles is very comfortably ensconced in London, I would say, from what I've seen today.'

'Yes, yes, but that wasn't quite what I meant. I suppose you wouldn't know. Not long after you left there was a— er—a disagreement between Charles and Judith. Until Edward went away Charles hadn't been back to the Manor for a couple of years.'

There was a pause, then Becky said slowly, 'Poor old Edward! I didn't know. It's odd, because I've met Charles on several occasions in France, and he never mentioned it.'

'I don't suppose he would. It's a family affair, after all, and you were hardly close as children.'

'I don't believe Charles was ever a child,' averred Becky.

Mrs Summerson was not deceived into thinking this a compliment. 'He had a very unfortunate upbringing,' she said excusingly. 'He was left too much in the care of servants while his father travelled. Edward should have re-married much earlier, when Charles needed a mother.'

Becky gave her an ironical look. 'That's your fairy-story mind again. You think Charles is a fairy prince *manqué*, don't you?'

Mrs Summerson bridled. 'No, no, I wouldn't say that. But he's—he would be,' she corrected herself, 'very attractive if he weren't so—so unpredictable.'

'Oh, Mother! You're the last of the Great Innocents. Look, Mother, fairy princes simply do not exist. Like the unicorn, they're fabulous beasts. And while I'm perfectly prepared to concede that Charles is frequently a beast . . .'

Her mother broke in laughing, 'All right, all right, I'm a hopeless romantic and I won't say another word. But you can't deny Charles' childhood was hardly happy.'

'I don't know,' objected her daughter. 'It may have been a trifle unorthodox by our standards, but he was desperately spoilt by devoted aunts and nannies and people. And Edward thought he was the cat's pyjamas.'

'Well, he could do all the things that Edward had never been able to,' said Mrs Summerson shrewdly. 'He rode, he fenced, he was clever, and Edward was very proud of him. That's why the quarrel was such a shame. Oh, Edward still saw him, of course—they used to meet in London. But Charles is so busy, and it seemed to me that they never had much time together. Charles always had to rush off somewhere.'

'The price of success,' said Becky lightly.

'I suppose so.' Mrs Summerson looked as if she thought the price too high. 'It used to upset Edward, I think, although of course he never said anything to me. And he missed Charles coming down here at weekends.'

'Well, he's his father,' said Becky excusingly. 'Even so, I find it difficult to believe that Edward went into a decline because Charles stopped coming to Almcote for the odd weekend.'

'He didn't go into a decline,' objected Mrs Summerson, giggling in spite of herself. 'You're too ridiculous! He had a heart attack, I told you. And it had nothing to do with Charles.'

'You amaze me.'

'Don't be unkind. Charles has been very good since his father's attack, and not least to you and me! It's not becoming of you to sneer at him.'

'I know it's not.' Becky was conscience-stricken. 'I'm sorry, Mother, it's just a little difficult ridding oneself of the habits of a lifetime. I keep forgetting that Charles has moved over from the enemy camp.'

'Well, don't,' her mother adjured her.

'I'll try. Do you want me to write out a hundred lines? *Charles is a Good Thing?* Not,' she added reflectively, 'that even you can say that. But tell me about Edward.' She was suddenly sober because, for all her teasing, she had been genuinely fond of Edward Mallory. 'What brought it on? Overwork?'

'In a way, I suppose. He's had angina for years and wasn't suppose to overdo it. But on this occasion I'm afraid it was Tessa.'

'*Tess?* What on earth has she been doing? Good lord, she's only a child.'

'No, she isn't. She's seventeen.'

'Ouch!' said Becky, making a face. 'I remember her when she was a kid with a ponytail, very excited about going to her new school. I haven't seen her more than a couple of times since then.'

'She's not so excited any more—she thinks she's too old to be at boarding school. She wants to leave and go to a sixth-form college, and Judith is bitterly opposed to it. That's why the trouble started.'

'But why?' demanded Becky blankly. 'What's wrong with a sixth-form college?'

'Nothing, except that Tess would live at home and Judith doesn't fancy having a grown-up daughter around all the time. It might,' said Mrs Summerson with a lapse from her usual charity, 'encourage people to do a few sums. Especially as Tessa is very—er—difficult to overlook.'

'Oh lord,' said Becky with feeling. 'How awful! Did Edward side with Tessa against her mother?'

'No, he was very fair. I think he'd have preferred her to be at home, but he didn't interfere when Judith said she had to go back to school last September. Perhaps he should have done—first of all she made a terrible nuisance of herself at school, and then she ran away.'

'I don't blame her,' said Becky stoutly. 'After all, as you say, she's not a child. There were girls of her age working in my office in Strasbourg. She's old enough to be listened to, especially about her own future.'

'Perhaps, but she's very stubborn when she gets an idea into her head. Just like her father. And it was sheer naughtiness to run away.'

Sympathising with the rebellious Tessa and perceiving that her mother didn't share the sentiment, Becky chuckled. 'It's probably what I'd have done in her place, always assuming I had the courage. Was that what upset Edward?'

'Oh no, that was nothing! The school wouldn't have her back, of course, and Judith said she wasn't going to be blackmailed into having her at home in such a fashion. And whatever you say,' added Mrs Summerson defiantly, 'I agree with her. You can't allow yourself to be terrorised by your children simply because they threaten to misbehave. Your life wouldn't be your own.'

'So what did Judith do?' asked Becky.

'She found her another school. I believe it's frightfully expensive, the sort of place parents send their children to as a last resort, and quite unsuitable for Tessa. She's mixing with all the wrong people. You know the sort of girl: too rich and too old for their years. And Tessa is naturally enough impressed by these girls. She's friendly with them, and because their families have money, Judith encourages it. She's been there since Christmas, and I hardly recognised her when she came home at Easter. She doesn't care for anyone any more, and she looks a *sight*. She's obviously got into the wrong company; she drinks too much, and the man who drove her home from school was nearly old enough to be her father—though he didn't behave like it.'

'Sounds nasty.'

'It was. And then, after Tessa went back for the summer term, Edward had his heart attack,' Mrs Summerson concluded.

'I'm not surprised. Lord, what a mess! I see what you mean—at least our problems would be solved by a pot of fairy gold, but nothing's going to reform Tessa or turn Judith into a loving mother. And it must fret Edward to leave them both to their own devices while he's in Switzerland.'

'It will fret him, I expect, but when he left he was too ill to bother about anything,' said Mrs Summerson sadly. 'And Charles has been very good. He'll do anything he can.'

'He can't turn himself into a loving mother for Tess, though. Poor kid, she must be very unhappy.'

Arrested, Mrs Summerson considered that carefully. 'I don't know. She seemed very pleased with herself at Easter.'

'Self-defence,' said Becky briefly, who knew something about the techniques of that art.

'It could be. I'm afraid I was so indignant about the way she treated her father that I didn't really think about her. She could be unhappy, I suppose,' mused her mother.

'I'd lay a substantial sum on it. Is she home now?'

'I wouldn't think so, unless it's half-term. And even if it is, she may have gone to stay with some of her new friends. Judith doesn't have her there more than she can help.'

'And Charles is hardly going to have her stay in London with him. He's not there half the time. I wonder,' mused Becky, 'if he was genuine when he said he wanted me to get to know Tess better? I'm hardly the maternal type, but at least I don't resent her as Judith seems to.'

'He wants you to get to know Tess better?' echoed Mrs Summerson in a peculiar tone.

Becky didn't notice. 'Yes, he seems really quite concerned for her—all rather out of character, I thought. To be honest, I suspected him of some dark plotting. He was talking of taking Tess away for a holiday at her half-term and wants me to go too.'

'Oh!' Mrs Summerson studied her daughter's face. 'And are you going?'

'He rather talked me into it,' admitted Becky. 'I don't see anything against it, though, do you?'

'That depends.'

'On what?'

'On how good you are with difficult teenagers,' her mother informed her brutally.

Becky was calm. 'I have no idea how good I may be, but I always used to like Tessa. Anyway, she's Charles' responsibility, not mine.'

'Yes, of course,' Mrs Summerson said hastily.

'That sounds very disbelieving,' observed Becky.

'It did just occur to me,' Mrs Summerson ventured, pleating her linen skirt absorbedly, 'that it might have been with some idea of delegating Tess to you that Charles invited you in the first place.'

Becky laughed. 'It's possible, I suppose! It didn't feel like that, though.'

Mrs Summerson looked up quickly. 'No?'

'No, not to me at any rate. It just sounded as if he felt that it was a fortunate coincidence that Tess and I were both available at the same time. He pointed out that I'd probably be in need of a holiday by the time I left France.'

Mrs Summerson was fascinated. 'Did he? And will you?'

'I imagine so,' Becky said, 'I didn't get away last year for a decent holiday.'

'And you think a holiday with Charles and Tessa will be restful?'

Becky was amused. 'Unlike you, obviously, I don't see why it shouldn't be.'

'Then perhaps it will,' said Mrs Summerson in a heartening tone. 'Where are you going?'

'I've left that to Charles,' said Becky carelessly. 'He had ideas on the subject and he seemed to know what he was doing.'

Her mother looked staggered. 'Er—I'm sure,' she said faintly. She stared at Becky in dawning amusement.

Discovering her mother's eyes on her, Becky put up her brows. 'What are you laughing at, Mama?'

'I? Oh, nothing.'

'What sort of nothing?' demanded Becky suspiciously.

'I was just thinking,' Mrs Summerson explained innocently, 'that Charles seems to have taken on rather a lot on your behalf.'

'And that's funny?'

'Perhaps not to you,' allowed Mrs Summerson, trying to control a quivering lip.

'*Not* to me,' Becky agreed, eyeing her mother with a certain hostility. 'I think you're being very silly.'

'I'm sure you do,' Mrs Summerson agreed sympathetically, and gave Becky a quick hug. 'And perhaps I am. I think I may have misjudged Charles,' she added with apparent irrelevance, then grew grave. 'I think perhaps we both have.'

Becky smiled at her affectionately. 'We did,' she corrected gently, 'we did indeed. But I think I have his motives cleared up now. He isn't fierce really—or rather he is, but not to us.'

'Not to *you*,' Mrs Summerson amended.

Becky chuckled. 'Well, I'm the only one who's had the courage to beard him so far!'

'Precisely,' interpolated Mrs Summerson, but she was not attended to.

'He would have been just as considerate to you if you'd gone to see him yourself.' And seeing her mother's look of disbelief, she insisted, 'Yes, he would.'

'He would have offered to take me away on holiday, of course,' agreed Mrs Summerson politely.

Becky opened innocent eyes wide. 'Oh, I'm sure, if he wants someone to keep an eye on Tessa.' She chuckled mischievously. 'I'm sure you'd do *that* much better than I shall!'

'You'll have your hands full,' opined Mrs Summerson. Once again her lips twitched. 'And so, unless I'm much mistaken, will Charles.'

CHAPTER FOUR

MUCH to Mrs Summerson's gratification, her second daughter elected to return to Orchard Cottage for the second time in as many weeks on Friday evening. She arrived before supper, wet and cold after her walk from the station. Mrs Summerson, as soon as she had greeted Chloe affectionately, retreated to the kitchen in a pre-occupied fashion. As a professional cook, Chloe put her on her mettle.

This left the sisters confronting one another over the log fire.

'Well,' said Chloe, spreading her fingers to the blaze, 'how are you?'

'Better, thank you.'

'Good.' Chloe surveyed her sister candidly. 'You were looking awfully seedy. You're not much better now.'

'Thank you,' said Becky with composure.

'I mean you look tired,' amended Chloe.

'I am tired. I've been to London.'

'Ah!' Chloe pounced. 'What happened?'

Becky looked prim. 'I was nearly battered to death on the Central Line. Really, the Underground gets worse every year! Either that or I've forgotten what it's like. One has functional memory lapses about unpleasant experiences, I suppose.'

'Don't,' said Chloe, 'be obtuse. I want to know about Charles.'

Becky chuckled. 'I'm sure you do,' she agreed sympathetically.

'So?'

'So nothing,' Becky sighed.

'You mean there aren't any new developments on the Mallory front?'

'None that need concern you,' she was told quite gently but with finality.

There was a disbelieving silence. Then Chloe said incredulously, 'Are you telling me to mind my own business?'

'I hoped not to have to put it so crudely,' shrugged Becky.

'But you're my *sister*,' pointed out Chloe.

'And you think I should have got used to your habit of not taking hints?'

Chloe grinned. 'You should have done by now,' she agreed, 'but what I meant was, you can't expect me not to be concerned about you.'

'I'm very grateful,' Becky assured her, her eyes twinkling.

'No, you're not. You're laughing at me.'

'The heavens forbid!'

'Yes, you are. And I don't mind,' Chloe said magnanimously. 'If you'll only ...' She broke off.

'Tell all?' supplied Becky, with a good deal of understanding.

'You always used to,' Chloe said sadly.

'That was a long time ago,' Becky reminded her, 'and it was mutual.'

Chloe stared. 'What do you mean?'

'I haven't noticed you rushing to confide in me all the details of the present state of your heart.' Becky flung up a hand as Chloe seemed about to interrupt. 'Don't misunderstand me, I don't want you to. Your life is your own affair, very properly. I merely wanted to point out that you don't feel the need to confide in me any more, any more than I do in you.'

'That's very hard,' mourned Chloe, looking as if she might weep.

Becky said gently, 'No it's not. It's natural. It's part of growing up. When you're young—or at least when I was young, I was never wholly sure of my own mind. So whenever there was a decision to be taken I used to go round to everyone I knew and talk about it. I didn't actually ask their advice, of course, it was much too degrading; but I did, by a roundabout way, discover their opinions. And having gleaned enough, I would make what I called my own decision on the basis of everything that had been said to me.'

Chloe was fascinated. 'And you've grown out of that?'

'Not altogether,' said Becky ruefully, 'perhaps I never will. I'm still never sure about whether I've made the right decision, once I've done it. I spend half my time looking backwards over my shoulder thinking, ah, but if I'd gone the other way ... Do you understand?'

'Yes,' said Chloe, 'yes, of course. But in that case I don't see why you don't want to discuss Charles. I mean, if you're not *sure* ...'

Becky looked amused. 'I'm not sure what *I* want to do, or whether *I've* done the right thing, but I'm quite sure what you want me to do.'

Chloe nibbled a fingertip reflectively. 'You *are* telling me to mind my own business.'

'Oh, very well, if that's the way you want to put it,' said Becky, losing patience.

'And you're really going to marry Charles?'

'Yes,' returned Becky, suddenly and inexplicably angry, 'I'm quite determined to do so.'

'Then you will,' said Chloe fatalistically.

Unseen by her, Becky superstitiously crossed her fingers, thinking even as she did so that it was a little late.

It was not only Chloe who disapproved of the marriage; Judith Mallory was far from pleased. Since her husband's enforced retirement to Switzerland she had led an ideal life, able to call upon Charles' advice and escort whenever she wanted it, licensed to ignore him whenever, as her undutiful daughter put it, she had other fish to fry. From Judith's point of view his acquisition of any wife was a distinct nuisance—her identity was a disaster.

Judith Mallory, having married a man old enough to be her father with a grown-up son barely five years younger than herself, had always, and not entirely fairly, been looked at askance in Almcote. Edward Mallory wasn't popular, but he was a substantial employer, and it was of some importance to the village what sort of woman he made his wife. In practice she turned out to be unhappy in the country and was seldom to be met at the Manor. Paradoxically this attracted a good deal of unwonted sympathy for her husband, who suddenly found himself more popular than he had ever been before.

To Judith this had been a matter of indifference, and soon after her only daughter was born she had abandoned any pretence of living at Almcote. She was by nature a restless creature, for ever planning new journeys with new acquaintances. For most of the year she travelled extensively, bowing only to convention in that she normally returned to Almcote for Christmas. Otherwise she was only to be seen at the Manor if she had a house-party, quitting it the moment the last of her guests had left.

Until her husband fell ill, this answered very well. Edward seldom accompanied her on her frequent trips to Paris or Rome, occasionally went with her to New York where he had business interests, and generally was content to let her go her own way. Tessa, in boarding school throughout the term, and happy enough at the

Manor where she had her beloved pony and plenty of children to play with during the holidays, fitted in admirably with her parents' way of life.

However, when Edward's angina was first diagnosed, his doctor had instructed Judith that he was to be kept quiet: early nights, peaceful days and a conservative diet were his recommendations. Judith fled to Nassau and Edward spent a fraught summer holiday with Tessa at the Manor, visited principally by Isabel Summerson, who had subsequently and most uncharacteristically taken it upon herself to rebuke Judith. It was therefore not wholly inexplicable that Mrs Mallory did not contemplate receiving Becky Summerson into the family with any degree of enthusiasm.

She summoned her daughter to expatiate and complain, and her description of Becky in particular was not flattering. Tessa, who remembered her only as a rather serious young woman reported by the village to be clever, was intrigued.

'Why did she go away?' she asked Judith. 'And stay away so long?'

'You may well ask,' said her mother maliciously.

Tessa knew the tone; it was one that Judith employed for retailing all her more sordid titbits of gossip. Tessa was was torn between distaste and an understandable curiosity.

'Blotted her copybook, did she?' she said, with that indifferent sophistication that infuriated her mother, partly because it was almost a carbon copy of her own social manner.

Judith shrugged, narrowing her eyes at her too worldly-wise daughter.

'Who knows? She used to be engaged to Edith Summerson's farm manager. Or at least that's what he called himself, though he never seemed to do much managing of anything except Becky. Of course, he must have thought she would inherit all Edith Summerson's property.'

'Oh!' Tessa digested this. 'Poor Becky.'

'Poor Becky, nothing—she asked for it. He was very dashing and she was quite devoted. It was the talk of the village. She'd never made even the smallest bit of a fool of herself before. We were all terribly surprised.'

'And pleased,' interpreted Tessa.

'It was not without its amusing side,' acknowledged Judith, 'especially as he had other—er—little traits.'

'Such as?'

'Oh, nothing one could pin down. When he first came he was very lively and good-looking, we were all rather glad to see a new face, to be honest. Almcote is so dull, and at least he livened it up a bit. Certainly nobody disliked him to begin with. Then people began to get suspicious. There were a series of small thefts; people would miss odd things, a bracelet here, a silver cream jug there. Things that might have been mislaid in an absent moment.'

'You mean this man took them?' Tessa's horror accorded ill with her pretensions to unshockability.

'Again, who knows?' Judith smiled to herself in a feline fashion. 'The thefts started shortly after he came and stopped the moment he left.'

'Did Becky know?'

Judith grinned. 'Becky? My darling, Becky is a lawyer. A thoroughly good, dull, boring creature, a positive pillar of the parish. I suspect she found out that the love of her life had been pilfering their little treasures from her friends, and fled the shame. Edith booted him out pretty quickly after Becky left, anyway.'

Tessa looked at her mother speculatively. 'Does Charles know?'

'That Becky prefers the criminal classes? I suppose so.

He was here, off and on, all that year. He's got ears and he's not stupid—— If I could work it out, so could he.'

'And doesn't he mind?'

'Mind what? That Becky used to be hooked on Tony Boyd? I don't see why he should.'

Tessa's head reared up. 'Tony Boyd?' she said, staring.

'Yes. He went off and married a *much* more lavish heiress—Megan Shepherd.'

'I know,' said Tessa shortly.

'Do you? Don't tell me you're mixed up with him too?' Judith sighed. 'Really, darling, where do you get hold of these dreary men? He's old enough to be your father.'

Tessa cast her a look of dislike and replied with composure, 'I've only met him a couple of times. His sister-in-law is at school with me.'

Judith surveyed her in dawning comprehension. 'Little Marina Shepherd? Is she Megan's sister? The people you stayed with at Easter?'

Tessa nodded.

'How amusing!' Judith stroked her chin thoughtfully. 'And they don't live all that far away either, do they? Perhaps we should ask them to the wedding; it might liven it up a bit.'

Tessa recoiled. '*Mother*! Charles would be furious.'

'To see Becky's past resurrected?' Judith considered it, half-laughing. 'I don't think he'd mind. Boyd is very prosperous—possibly unlawfully.'

'Well, surely he'd mind that,' pointed out Tessa, 'even if he's not consumed with jealousy. Though I don't see why you're so certain he wouldn't be—— After all, he's *marrying* Becky.'

'Don't be such a little monster,' said Judith pettishly. 'If you really want to know why your brother is suddenly plunging into matrimony, you should look a little nearer home.'

Tessa was understandably blank.

'I suspect,' said Judith with exaggerated patience, 'that it's because of you.'

'Me?' Tessa, who had carefully piled her long hair on top of her head and was admiring herself in the several mirrors on her mother's dressing table, spun round, the suddenly loosened hair flying. '*Me?*' she repeated. 'But why?'

Judith laughed softly. 'You've made such an unholy nuisance of yourself, my darling, and I'm afraid Charles wrote me off as an incompetent mother years ago. Now, with Daddy non-combatant as it were, Charles thinks you're a bit short of desirable influences. And whatever else Rebecca Summerson may be,' she mused, 'she is an indubitably good influence.' She showed her teeth. 'Like her mother.'

Tessa was no fool and had, besides, witnessed the preliminaries when Isabel Summerson had taken her mother to task. Nevertheless, the idea that Charles might be set on providing her with a mentor did not seem unreasonable, given his previous attitude. In particular Tessa recalled a pungent address to her on the subject of her lifestyle and companions at the time of her father's departure for Switzerland.

'I don't believe it,' she said uncertainly.

Judith shrugged. 'You'll find out,' she said cryptically.

Tessa's face creased. 'I don't believe Charles would do a thing like that. It's cheating.'

'I don't see why,' objected her mother. 'Anyway, if he wanted to marry the girl he could have done so any time this last five years, I dare say, but he didn't. And he wouldn't have done so now if you hadn't forced his hand. It's too boring of you!'

Tessa looked resentful. 'I don't believe it,' she repeated sullenly, 'there's no point. I mean, I come of age in a year, and then Charles can't do anything, even if he wants to.'

'He might consider it worth marrying the girl for a year on the remote chance that she may reform you in that time,' pondered Judith. 'After all, there's always divorce.'

Tessa sprang up. 'That's horrible!'

Her mother hid a smile. 'Oh, I agree with you, my poor darling, a ghastly prospect. He may let you leave school, but I bet you'll find yourself living with her instead. You'll end up tending the poor or something if you don't look out for yourself. She's a great one for good works, I imagine the whole family is. No doubt that's how Charles has presented you to her: as a helpless waif. You must seem a very suitable object for her charity.'

The words bit. Tessa was not unaware of her mother's malice and was shrewd enough to discount a good deal that she said; nevertheless, Becky was a stranger and the prospect before her not a very reassuring one.

'I don't believe Charles would behave like that,' she insisted. 'You judge everyone by yourself. Charles wouldn't marry someone as a convenience.'

Judith's eyes narrowed. 'I won't have you speaking to me like that, Tessa.'

Her daughter glared at her.

'I'll have an apology,' Judith said in a steely voice. She stood up. 'Don't stand there and defy me. Apologise!'

Tessa held her eyes steadily, without speaking, and Judith slowly sat down again.

'Oh well, it's quite amusing,' she said indolently. 'Though why you should suddenly have developed this hero-worship for Charles I can't imagine. He's no plaster saint.'

'I never thought he was,' objected Tessa, whose admiration for her remote half-brother was of long but hitherto concealed standing.

'Good! At least you'll be spared the disillusion.'

Tessa suddenly looked very world-weary, an expression which chilled Judith. To have so sophisticated a daughter was, she felt, a particularly cruel stroke of fate.

'I don't think,' said Tessa ruefully, 'that I have many illusions, Mother.' She paused. 'About anybody,' she added, as she drifted away to her own room.

Judith found she had nothing to say.

Saturday morning found both Tessa Mallory and her prospective sister-in-law harried from their beds at an early hour to go visiting. Of the two Tessa, more curious than Becky, was the easier to rouse. Becky herself, who had been persuaded by a persistent mother that it would be an impermissible unkindness to leave Almcote without paying at least a courtesy call on Great-Aunt Edith, was more recalcitrant.

In fact, Becky was sitting glumly in the window seat of the sitting room, surveying a day which had, with miraculous treachery, suddenly turned sunny, when Tessa arrived. She greeted Tessa's advent as a reprieve.

'Come in,' she urged her warmly. 'Coffee? Or would you rather have a drink?'

Mrs Summerson frowned heavily, but Becky rose rapidly in Miss Mallory's estimation. She was not, however, prepared to admit it. While she was by no means convinced by her mother's arguments, Tessa had considerable and not unfounded reservations about Charles' future wife. She was favourably impressed by the unaffected pleasure with which Becky had greeted her, but experience of adults had taught her to be wary. Miss Summerson had to be shown that Miss Mallory was not to be flattered into submission, so she responded to the hospitable invitation coolly.

'Nothing, thank you,' she said, keeping Becky in her place. 'I only came over because Mother said I ought to.'

Mrs Summerson's eyebrows rose, and Becky, who had not been prepared for rudeness, was disconcerted. She began to consider Tessa as something other than a heaven-sent excuse to put off going to see Aunt Edith, and her heart sank.

Surveying her frankly, Becky decided that Tessa had not done well from her family inheritance. There was no trace of her mother's fine bone-structure and hawk-like elegance of movement; Tessa had her father's features, too strong for prettiness, but very striking. She was very tanned, a fact which cheesecloth blouse and brief shorts had done nothing to disguise, and Mrs Summerson did not try to hide her disapproval. It was a deliberately childish costume, but there was nothing about Tessa—even with her hair in bunches and her feet bare—that suggested a child. She looked a complete urchin, but a worldly-wise one. Becky, taking in the enormous eyes equally sophisticated and wary, and the expert maquillage which decorated them, began to feel sorry for herself. Tessa looked both petulant and strong-willed, and Becky had all but agreed to take her on holiday.

'No doubt,' said Becky ironically, 'your mother thought it would be a good idea for us to get acquainted.'

Tessa looked at her sharply, suspecting a double edge to the remark and not wholly certain of her ground. She took refuge in sulks. 'I wouldn't know.'

'No? Well, perhaps you wouldn't.' Becky searched for some topic of mutual interest and at last managed a little desperately, 'Are you on holiday from school?'

Tessa was scornful. 'No, I've only just gone back. I got a weekend exeat because Mother phoned and said she wanted me home. I ought,' with conscious martyrdom, 'to be working on my German.'

'German? Oh yes, I remember Charles told me you were doing exams. What are they? "A" Levels?'

The rouged face settled into deeper sullen lines. 'No, "O's" I failed last summer.'

Oh dear, thought Becky ruefully, but she managed to say in a tone which she hoped was both sympathetic and disinterested, 'Tedious for you.'

'I'm too old to be at school,' said Tessa loudly and aggressively.

'Quite a lot of people are still at school at your age,' Becky pointed out.

'I,' Tessa informed her, 'am old for my age.'

Becky found she could believe it.

'School is, however, quite a good place from which to take exams,' she offered judicially. 'If you're interested, that is. How much longer have you got before they start?'

Tessa shuddered. 'Three weeks.'

'And how long do they go on for?'

'A fortnight, and then there's nothing to do, but I've still got to stay at school until the end of term. It's such a waste!'

Becky was inclined to agree, but judged that to do so would only convince Tessa that she was trying to curry favour. 'But it will be nice to have a free summer, won't it?' she said. 'I always used to have a wonderful sense of freedom after I'd finished my exams, I remember.'

'You,' said Tessa drily, 'were probably free.'

Becky laughed. 'I certainly thought I was! I've always had a great respect for personal freedom.'

There was a brief not unsympathetic silence during which Becky thought she could detect signs of softening on Tessa's part. It was, however, quickly dispelled by the sound of tyres swishing to a bad-tempered halt outside the gates of Orchard House. Looking out idly, she was amazed to see Charles, his face like a thundercloud, getting out of the car.

Instantly Tessa jumped up.

'I suppose he's come for me,' she said resignedly. 'I knew he'd go berserk when he found Mother had brought me down from school. I told her, but she wouldn't listen.'

She left, without apology or farewell.

Mrs Summerson exchanged a sneaking look with her daughter.

'What a dreadful child,' she said. 'You can't possibly take her on, Becky! She looks about thirty with all that stuff on her face.'

'Don't be hidebound, Mama,' returned Becky, 'presumably it washes off. I doubt whether it's indelible.'

'If she washes,' sniffed Mrs Summerson, determined to look on the black side. 'Becky, *think*. She's too grown up and too clever. There was a time when she was simply a neglected little girl and I was sorry for her; she had no manners, but you can deal with that if you're firm enough. But since she's been at that school, she's changed. Well, you heard her! She thinks she knows all the answers.'

'Perhaps she does,' said Becky tranquilly. 'Some of them, anyway.'

Mrs Summerson looked disturbed. 'Once you start thinking like that, you've lost the battle.'

'I hope that there isn't going to be any battle.'

'Don't be silly,' said her mother. 'If there weren't any battle, Charles wouldn't need a champion, and if he didn't need a champion he wouldn't have got engaged to you. Would he?'

Becky was downcast. 'I suppose not.'

Her mother took her hand and patted it. 'Poor love, I don't mean to nag you. But I do think you've got yourself into a rather equivocal position, and I don't think you realise how difficult it's going to be. Tessa is more than difficult, and I've no doubt her mother has been encouraging her to rebel. Don't forget Judith has little reason to love us. It's going to be a hard six months for you if Charles is going to hold you to that iniquitous bargain. Tessa will resent you, Judith will probably behave as badly as she can, and I shall be very surprised if you get any support at all from Charles.'

Becky bit her lip. 'Everything you say may well be true,' she admitted, 'but I can't help seeing that I owe Charles a debt. And he's been very chivalrous.'

'Possibly,' said Mrs Summerson, sounding like Chloe, 'but look at his ulterior motive.'

'As to ulterior motives,' retorted Becky, 'what about my own?'

'My debt,' diagnosed Mrs Summerson.

Becky was confused. 'No, of course not, I didn't mean that. I shouldn't have said it. I didn't think.'

'I knew you were doing this for me,' said Mrs Summerson sadly. 'You were always like that, from a child. You've always wanted to look after other people, particularly incompetents like me. But there are some lengths to which you shouldn't go, even for family. You should never have let yourself be blackmailed into becoming engaged to that man. Although, of course,' she added fondly, 'I love you for it.'

There was a slight sound from the French window and they looked up to see Charles standing silhouetted against the May garden. There was no sign on his face that he had heard their conversation, but Becky had the oddest impression not only that he had, but that Mrs Summerson's innocent shafts had gone home.

Conscience-stricken, she got up and went towards him with her hands out in a more welcoming gesture than he had ever yet received from her. He looked at her for a moment, unsmiling, before he took her hands.

'Charles! I thought you'd come to collect Tessa.'

'You mean Tessa thought I'd come to collect Tessa. I've never seen such a blatant guilty conscience.'

'Because she wasn't at school? I don't think,' said Becky tentatively, 'that it was wholly her fault.'

He gave her an ironic look. 'I am aware. God knows what Judith thinks she's about! We shall have the devil of a fight on her hands if the little wretch goes and fails her exams all over again.'

'Perhaps she's not academically inclined,' ventured Becky, 'some people aren't, you know.'

He laughed grimly. 'Innocent Becky! There's none of that about Tessa. She's as sharp as they come, she's just lazy, and her mother encourages her. I sometimes wonder if Judith thinks that as long as Tessa goes on failing exams she'll have to stay at school.'

He gave a quick impatient sigh and pressed her fingers. She became aware that he was still holding her hands and drew them from his grasp, blushing. He looked at her suddenly, as if he had forgotten briefly where they were, and let her go with a slight laugh. Her brow creased in concern at his evident worry.

'Don't look like that.' He uncreased her forehead with soothing fingers. 'It's my problem. There's no need for you to disturb yourself.'

'How can I help it?' she protested. 'You asked for my help.'

He was instantly rueful. 'I did, didn't I? I'm not sure that was altogether fair of me.'

So he had heard her conversation with her mother.

'Nonsense,' she said briskly. 'Even if I hadn't let my tongue run away with me last week, surely we're sufficiently old friends to be able to ask each other for help?'

96

Charles looked wry. 'Would you call us old friends?'

Becky was mischievous. 'When I'm being charitable.'

'And you're charitable quite a lot of the time, aren't you?' His expression was compounded of exasperation, mockery and something else that she could not identify, but disturbed her.

'It's extremely irritating,' he told her. 'It makes you quite—unassailable.'

She laughed. 'I wish you'd tell Tessa that! She found me perfectly assailable.'

'Ah, but she's still at that innocent age when anybody who stands in the way you want to go is automatically an enemy, even if they do it for impeccably moral reasons.'

'What you mean,' said Mrs Summerson from where she stood behind Becky, in a voice full of suppressed rage, 'is that Tessa is a self-willed little monster who is going to make Becky's life hell.'

Charles, almost as a deliberate insult to her mother, thought Becky, possessed himself of her hands again and walked into the room.

'Oh, not her life,' he drawled, 'just the next six months or so.'

Mrs Summerson gave a squeak of outrage. 'And you're not going to lift a finger,' she accused.

'I'm not going to start beating Tessa at this late stage,' he agreed, amused.

Mrs Summerson peered at him. 'And you're really proposing to make Becky take that child on holiday?'

'More than proposing. That's what I've come about,' he looked down at Becky, smiling, 'at least in part.'

'Having despatched Tessa back to school, suitably chastened,' she nodded.

His face closed. 'As you say,' he said smoothly. 'Chastened and bribed. I told her any more playing truant, even

97

at Judith's instigation, and she didn't come with us—which should prove effective, as she's been wanting to come to the island for a long time.'

'Island?' queried Becky.

He raised his eyebrows. 'You don't mean you're actually interested?' he teased, not altogether pleasantly.

She was confused. 'Well, of course I am, if that's where you're taking Tessa. Unless you've changed your mind about having me along, of course,' she added conscientiously.

There was a little silence while Mrs Summerson held her breath.

Then Charles said lightly, 'Far from it. The thought of being incarcerated with Tessa for fifteen days makes me positively suicidal. You can't back out now, anyway, my secretary has booked what she assures me is an incredibly complicated journey. If I asked her to change the tickets now I think she'd hand in her notice. And Annabella is far too valuable for me to let her go, so you'll oblige me by being ready by the twenty-second of June.'

He turned to go, nodding briefly at Mrs Summerson and raising a negligent hand to Becky.

'But where are we going?' she demanded, flustered. 'I mean, what do I take with me? Where do I meet you? How long will we be travelling? Charles, you are the most exasperating man! You can't just walk out like that.'

'Yes, I can,' he averred, his temper apparently restored. 'I have to take Tessa back to school, remember. As for where we meet—phone my secretary. I leave all the details to her. You'll find her very efficient.'

'And I'm to do just what she says?'

'Unless you want to drive her away from me.' He swung neatly back to face her. 'In which case,' he said sweetly, 'I should be very, very cross.'

CHAPTER FIVE

Becky, feeling that her letter of resignation needed a certain personal softening, flew back to Strasbourg on Sunday night. In the meantime she had tried without success to contact Charles or his unknown secretary. It irked her to know no more of Charles' plans than he had chosen to throw at her casually as he left Orchard House, and she brooded on his perversity for the rest of the weekend.

She was, however, a diligent and conscientious employee, and nine o'clock on Monday morning found her at her desk, all thought of the irritating Mr Mallory banished once she had asked her secretary to book a personal call to him in London.

After an hour or so, when she was beginning to flag, there was a perfunctory knock on her door and a pleasant-faced man strode in and found her almost invisible behind a stack of files.

'Good lord,' he exclaimed, halting on the threshold. 'What on earth are you doing? Making a nest with waste paper?'

Becky giggled. 'I'm trying to put things in order.'

'Why?' He shut the door and lounged against it. 'You've never bothered before.'

'That's not kind,' she retorted. 'I can always find things.'

'I don't dispute it. Which surely makes this new efficiency drive of yours a little unnecessary, if not worse. When papers are in their rightful place in the system,' he pointed out not unreasonably, 'in all probability you *won't* be able to find them.'

'Yes, but you will. I've never met such a well-organised man.'

'That sounds like a death-knell,' he observed ruefully. 'Becky, will you stop raising all this dust and come out and tell me what you're doing?'

She emerged, not altogether unwillingly.

'I'm putting my house in order,' she said calmly. 'I thought you'd have got my letter, John; I posted it at the same time as I did my resignation. Presumably it's lost somewhere in the internal circulation. I'm sorry.'

John Townsend looked staggered. 'Resignation?' he repeated stupidly. 'Do you mean you're leaving?'

'That's the general idea.' Becky cleared a space on the office's only comfortable chair and sat down in it. 'Ugh! Paper is filthy stuff,' she remarked, staring at her own grey fingertips.

He ignored the rider. 'Why?'

She shifted her shoulders. 'Oh, lots of reasons. My contract is up, anyway, and I thought perhaps I'd leave before they got round to throwing me out.'

'Oh, nonsense,' he said impatiently, 'your work is excellent. You'd have been promoted this year—I'm moving out of the Legal Department and there can't be much doubt that you would get my job. What on earth's going to happen to the Department if we both go?'

Becky gave her warm chuckle. 'It will get a radical new look. Isn't that what the latest Mission Circular said was needed anyway? All departments should radically review their procedures.' She made a face at the pompous phrase.

'You're not rushing at this, are you?' he said doubtfully. 'I mean, you went dashing off on this leave of yours with virtually no warning. At the time I thought that wasn't like you, but we all get restless. I mean, we wouldn't be human if we didn't. It's a very good thing as long as one doesn't take it too far. After all, this is your career, and you don't want to throw it all up on the spur of the moment and regret it later. Have you really thought about what you're doing?'

Becky had by now become so used to the idea that her job in Strasbourg was a minor irritant of which she should divest herself as soon as possible that she was momentarily disconcerted.

'Not quite in those terms, no,' she agreed. 'But there are other circumstances.'

'In what way?'

'Oh, personal circumstances. The situation that called me home so unexpectedly was more complicated than I bargained for.' She looked at her watch. 'In fact I'm expecting a call at any moment from someone to settle the minor details.'

His eyes narrowed. 'Would the someone be male?'

She gave him a quick look. He wasn't a possessive man, but there had long been a slightly proprietorial tone in his voice when he spoke to or of her friends. Becky wondered briefly if he could be jealous and discounted the possibility at once.

'He would,' she said lightly.

'And you wait on his pleasure before going home?'

'In this case,' she said ruefully, 'I don't have much choice. I have to see him and he's very busy. I just hope he can fit me in somewhere.'

'He sounds like a Cabinet Minister.'

She laughed. 'No doubt he will be one day, but at the moment he's a simple barrister. Very clever. Very rude.'

John Townsend regarded her seriously. 'Sounds just your type. An old friend?'

'Well, yes, I suppose so, but not in the way you mean.'

'And which way is that?'

She primmed her mouth, looking censorious. 'My shameful past.'

His eyes narrowed. 'Oh, have you got a shameful past? I must say I've always wondered. Your present is so spectacularly blameless.'

There was a faint edge to his tone, and Becky stopped laughing. 'So is my past,' she assured him briskly, 'too boring for words.'

'And the rude barrister?'

'Well, you probably wouldn't call him boring,' Becky said fairmindedly, 'but I've known him since I was eight years old, and the novelty has rather worn off.'

Townsend was relieved, and unguarded enough to show it. 'Oh, a father figure.'

Becky's eyebrows flew up. 'Er—possibly,' she agreed, a look of secret amusement curling her mouth.

He was concerned. 'Look, I don't want to interfere—but when your sister turned up in Strasbourg I wondered—I mean, if there's anything wrong at home, let me help if I can.'

At once all the amusement disappeared, and for a moment she looked at him thoughtfully. It would be the same as always, he saw at once. Whenever one approached too closely she threw up a protective screen. It was not that she was rude or even chilly; she was merely polite. He knew it so well, that expression on her face: always civil, always sweet, and quite unmoved.

'Thank you,' she said composedly. 'By the way, Chloe asked me to convey her apologies when next I saw you. She hadn't realised what a heinous crime it was to invade the Section without clearance. She said to say that she hoped she hadn't embarrassed you with the hierarchy.'

John Townsend looked amused. 'She embarrassed you rather than me, I would have said. After all, you had to be called out of a meeting to identify her. Did you take her to task?'

'Good lord, no, I didn't worry about it,' said Becky

lightly. 'I thought it was good for the security to have a little jolt for once. Keeps them on their toes. It just goes to show they're not as perfect as they like to think they are. If Chloe could get into the building, so could somebody much less desirable. Even so, they only caught up with her because she went to the English delegation as she said she was going to. If she'd gone to one of the other delegations or into the cellars or something, she'd have been lost without trace.'

He shuddered. 'Don't talk about it,' he begged. 'That isn't the reason for your sudden decision to leave, is it?'

Becky laughed. 'Oh really, John. What an idea! I thought the whole thing was a storm in a teacup except that it was quite amusing—they'd hardly throw me out because my sister chatted up the commissionaire. Or it hadn't occurred to me that they would, at any rate,' she added thoughtfully.

'No,' he smiled reluctantly, 'but it did make things a little awkward. Security aren't exactly pleased with you—or indeed any of us.'

'The French passion for authority,' Becky dismissed it in what he privately thought was an unduly insouciant manner. She gave her mischievous chuckle. 'If they try to make trouble I should circulate a report on the inadequacy of their security arrangements. You mustn't let them get you down, John.'

'It's not that easy,' he said gloomily. 'I've been doing things like this all my life. It's all very well for you, you're comparatively new to it.'

'I've been here two years,' objected Becky.

He snorted. 'Two years! That's nothing. I was six years in Washington before I went to The Hague, and I spent nearly ten years there before this job. I'm so entrenched in organisational protocol I've begun to write memos to myself.'

'Oh, I do that all the time,' Becky told him airily. 'I think the sooner I leave the better.'

John stopped laughing at that. 'Are you quite sure?' he said gravely.

Her telephone rang. She paused before answering it.

'Quite sure,' she told him. 'This job was never much more than an escape hatch for me—I'm basically a domestic beast, and it's time I went back to my own burrow. I've been running away too long. I must go back and square up to things.'

He raised a hand in a gesture of surrender. 'You know your own business best,' he returned in a tone which meant just the opposite. 'I'll see you later.'

She nodded at him, saying into the telephone, 'Rebecca Summerson.'

It was her secretary. 'Your call to London, Miss Summerson. Mr Mallory is in Leeds. Will you talk to a Miss Smart?'

'If she'll talk to me,' replied Becky, 'thank you, Janet.'

Annabella Smart sounded quite as efficient as Charles had made her out to be. Becky had no need to identify herself and ask any of the questions she had prepared. Miss Smart clearly had not only Charles' itinerary but her own and Tessa's readily to hand. She spoke briskly and to the point, and Becky had a hard task to scribble all the admirably precise details down on her notepad as Miss Smart dictated them. She had a momentary regret that she had not asked Janet to listen in and take them down in shorthand. She was quite certain that if there were any mistake about the arrangements it would be her fault for omitting some essential piece of information from her jotting.

'And the flight leaves for Istanbul at half-past three in the afternoon,' concluded Miss Smart. 'Mr Mallory will meet you on the plane if he doesn't manage to contact you in the airport lounge. He has a very heavy schedule at that end of the week, but he should make it. And your seat and Miss Mallory's have been reserved.'

'Er—thank you,' said Becky, scribbling feverishly. 'Istanbul?'

'There will be other transport to take you on from there,' Miss Smart responded distantly. 'Mr Mallory will be with you by then and he will keep the relevant papers. I have mailed your tickets for the flight out to,' she must have consulted some record because there was a pause before she read out '—to Orchard House, Almcote. Is that right?'

'Thank you,' said Becky again, weakly. She was tempted to ask where they were going after Istanbul, having no doubt that Miss Smart would know, but her pride revolted. She was about to put the telephone down, saying 'Goodbye,' when she was interrupted.

'And the second item Charles, I mean Mr Mallory, asked me to brief you on, is the negotiations between Mrs Summerson and one of his father's companies. I believe you know the details.'

Miss Smart managed to make them sound incredibly sordid.

'Yes, I do.'

'He asked me to say he has written to Mrs Summerson, explaining that it is the personal wish of his father that the arrangement be terminated as it now stands. That means, of course, that there is no question of further repayment by Mrs Summerson or her agents.'

'But that's impossible——' began Becky involuntarily. She began to perceive why Charles hadn't wanted to discuss the matter with her. He knew she would never agree to what amounted to downright charity, and nor would her mother, when she eventually floundered her way through the incomprehensible phraseology in which he had no doubt couched his communication.

'That was the message,' responded Miss Smart frigidly, as if Becky had cast doubts on her veracity. 'Should you wish to take up the matter with Mr Mallory personally, I can ask him to call you.' It did not sound as if she placed any reliance on his doing so.

'That won't be necessary, thank you,' replied Becky, pulling herself together. 'Thank you for the information. I shall speak ... that is, I shall no doubt be in touch with Charles without putting you to that trouble.'

'Very well.' Was there a hint of laughter in the smooth tones? 'Then you don't wish me to leave any message for Mr Mallory?'

'No, thank you. Goodbye.'

Again she was forestalled.

'May I take this opportunity,' purred Miss Smart, managing to sound both unctuous and slightly scornful, 'to wish you every happiness in your engagement? I wasn't in the office on Friday, when I understand the rest of the staff had the chance to offer their congratulations.'

'Oh!' said Becky blankly. She remembered that Charles had said chambers was a feudal society, and had taken it for an amusing exaggeration. 'Thank you,' she answered awkwardly, 'you're very kind.'

'Not at all,' disclaimed Miss Smart. 'And I hope you enjoy your holiday.'

She rang off briskly.

Becky slowly replaced the telephone, feeling somewhat stunned. Miss Smart's efficiency was literally breath-taking. No wonder Charles was reluctant to lose her. And yet there was a faintly uncomfortable suggestion that Miss Smart was in command of more than her employer's business affairs. Brows knit, Becky sank a thoughtful chin into her clasped hands. Could there be some further, closer relationship between them? And if so, why did he not ask Annabella Smart to take Tessa under her wing? She sounded more than capable of the task, and there would then have been no need to involve *her*. The more she thought about it, the more puzzled Becky became.

In the end she abandoned her thoughts and her devastated office and went to the refectory on the first floor for a cup of coffee.

There she found her secretary, Janet Hardy, and John Townsend already ensconced at a table by the window. This in itself was sufficiently surprising to raise her eyebrows. John was far from unapproachable, but the hierarchy within the organisation usually maintained rigid status at meals as well as within the office. Janet would normally no more have thought of taking her coffee with Miss Summerson's superior that John would have thought of inviting her to do so.

On this occasion, however, Janet had sought him out. It had long been the practice of the readers in the news room to pass on out-of-date newspapers to other offices when they had once been perused for official news. Today Janet had begun to look at last week's copies of *The Times* and had seen, almost without believing it, the curt announcement of the engagement between Mr Charles Edward Mallory, Q.C., of Almcote, Wiltshire and Miss Rebecca Jane Summerson of Strasbourg. It had seemed to her, for she was a kind girl, that it was imperative to communicate this to Mr Townsend before he discovered it from some less sympathetic source. Janet had worked for Miss Summerson ever since she came to Strasbourg and had been John Townsend's secretary before that; and she was very well aware, although Miss Summerson appeared not to be, that Mr Townsend was more closely attached to his assistant than the job warranted or excused.

John had been grateful but not, to Janet's amazement, altogether surprised.

'I thought it must be something like that,' he said resignedly, folding the offending page over and pushing it away from him. Absentmindedly he sugared his coffee for the third time. 'Did she tell you, Miss Hardy?'

'No, I just happened to see it in the paper. I suppose there can't be any doubt? It is our Miss Summerson?'

'Oh, no possible doubt. She could,' he said wistfully, 'have told us herself.'

Janet Hardy was uncomfortable. 'She probably didn't want any fuss. You know what it's like when someone leaves to get married. Miss Summerson wouldn't like that.'

'No,' he agreed. 'She's told you she's leaving, then?'

'She did just mention it when she asked me to help tidy her files this morning. Said there was a lot to do in four weeks.'

'There must be,' he said miserably. 'It's amazing the stuff you acquire without noticing. And she's been here a goodish while. It won't be the same when she's gone, will it?'

'There'll be somebody else,' said heartening Miss Hardy, 'probably just as nice. I think Miss Summerson is doing the right thing.'

'So does she,' he said ruefully. 'She thinks she was getting into a rut.'

'Perhaps she was. And anyway, I think the younger people marry the better. You want to have your family while you're young. Plenty of time to come back to your career after the children are grown up,' opined Miss Hardy. 'Not that Miss Summerson's a schoolgirl, but you know what I mean. Once she'd made up her mind, I think she's right not to hang about for ages before they marry.'

Townsend winced. 'It never occurred to me that she'd

marry,' he said unguardedly. 'She always seemed so—so aloof somehow.' He looked up into Miss Hardy's kind eyes and gave a bitter little laugh. 'Oh, I never got to first base with her,' he said. 'I never knew anyone else that did either, though I know quite a few people have tried one way or another. I suppose I just got into the habit of assuming she was immune. Silly of me. Now I shall have to train another assistant all over again. It will delay my move, too.'

Miss Hardy was relieved at the change of subject and they were well into inter-departmental gossip by the time Becky caught sight of them. Becky was shrewd enough to suspect that she had been, at least initially, the topic of their mutual interest and promptly decided not to linger in the refectory, thereby embarrassing both her colleagues and herself, and skirting their table, she threw them a cordial smile.

'Can't stop,' she remarked, 'my office looks as if it's been riding the whirlwind.'

John Townsend jumped to his feet, leaving his cold and over-sweetened coffee on the table. 'I'll come with you. We didn't finish our conversation, if you remember.' He nodded to Janet Hardy as they left.

In her office, he said, 'They tell me you're engaged, Becky.'

She sat very still. At last she said coolly, 'Janet has been gossiping, I infer.'

'On the contrary, any indiscretions were all mine.'

'How disconcerting,' she said coldly.

'Oh, for God's sake stop fencing with me, Becky,' he snapped.

'I wasn't aware that I was.'

He flung away from her furiously and thumped his hand down hard on the corner of her desk.

'You are the most unspeakably infuriating woman …'

He stopped and strove for calm. 'Look, my dear, I only want to help you.'

'To do what?'

'Whatever you want to do, I suppose,' he said tiredly. 'O.K., it's none of my business, I know. You don't even have to say it any more. I'll go.'

Becky's voice stopped him. 'No, don't. I'm sorry, John. I didn't mean to be ungrateful. You're very kind—too kind. I don't deserve it.'

He turned to her. 'Deserving doesn't normally come into these things,' he said wryly. 'Oh, my dear, you know . . .'

But she prevented him, with one hand flung up in an instinctive gesture of rejection.

'I wish you wouldn't get so involved, John.'

'I know you do,' he rested both his arms on the safe and considered her troubled face kindly, 'you've never made any secret of it. What I don't understand is why. Because it's not just me, is it? It's everyone. Nobody is allowed to care for you. *Why?*'

She shrugged. 'Because I can't give anything back, if you must know.'

He pounced on it. 'Can't? Or won't?'

She turned away impatiently. 'It comes to the same thing, doesn't it?'

'Not always. I used to wonder sometimes if you were already married.' When she didn't answer, he asked outright, 'Is that it?' He paused hopefully, then, 'Well then, you were married? Some sort of acrimonious divorce has soured you and made you eschew men for ever.'

She chuckled at his melodramatic tone. 'I've hardly managed to eschew you,' she pointed out.

'No divorce?'

'Oh, you're too ridiculous,' she exclaimed between

laughter and annoyance. 'I was engaged. A long time ago, before I came to France even.'

'And?'

'And it was broken off. Q.E.D.'

'He jilted you?'

She wrinkled her nose. 'Not a very complimentary way of putting it. No, he didn't, as a matter of fact, although I've no doubt he would have done eventually. In fact it was I who ended it. But it was all very messy and distasteful, and I prefer not to think about it.' Her tone was quite final.

'Q.E.D.,' he mused.

'Satisfied?'

'Oh, entirely,' he said ironically. 'Is he the man you're going to marry? This—what's his name?—Mallory?'

'Good lord, no.' Becky looked uncomfortable. 'It's not that sort of affair at all.'

'Is it not?' He looked suddenly eager. 'That's the man you were calling this morning, wasn't it? Mallory? You said,' he was accusing, 'that it was a family matter.'

'So it is.' She passed a weary hand over her brow. 'Look, John, I can see I should have told you about this myself, and I'm sorry. It's a private matter and I don't want to discuss it, but I do regret not telling you. It just slipped my mind. That's my only excuse.'

'It—slipped—your—mind?'

'Well, I've had a lot to think about one way and another, what with clearing up in the office and packing at home, and having my things shipped back to England.'

'So that your future husband gets overlooked. Quite understandable.'

She laughed, not very happily. 'Well, he isn't among my *immediate* problems.'

John Townsend shook his head. 'Curiouser and curiouser.'

'What is?'

'You,' he told her. 'When Janet Hardy told me you were engaged I thought, ah well, that's that. There's been this man in the background as long as we've known her and that accounts for everything. Now he's decided he wants her back and the rest of us can go hang.'

'It's not like that,' began Becky.

'No, I can see it's not,' he agreed soberly, 'which is why I said curiouser and curiouser. The mystery remains.'

She snorted. 'What mystery?'

'The Becky Summerson mystery. The girl who ran away from home because she broke an engagement; the girl who's kept running in case she got involved again.'

Alarm flared in her eyes.

'John——'

He straightened and said very quietly, 'I told you I wanted to marry you a year ago; I haven't told you again because you have effectively prevented me. But I've wanted to, and I still do. Go home. Go back to your sister and this rude father figure of yours, if that's what you think you want. Go and sort out your problems if you can. But if you can't, I shall be here, whenever you want me. Remember that.'

'No,' she said sharply. 'No, John, I can't let you ...'

The telephone shrilled and she picked it up.

'Damn,' she said with concentrated fury, and to him, 'No, don't go.'

It was Janet. 'I'm sorry to disturb you, Miss Summerson, but the Assistant Principal's on the line. I said I'd see if you were in.'

'Oh, very well,' said Becky irritably, 'put her through.'

Townsend opened the door.

'John, please,' she called out, but he left without turning his head.

Neither of them referred to the conversation again, and in the office they actually saw little of each other during Becky's last weeks. Townsend was fully occupied in helping to recruit her successor while Becky worked late evening after evening to finish any job that might prove difficult or obscure to a new assistant.

'The new man will think it's a very dull post,' she told Janet Hardy ruefully. 'I've tidied up all the really interesting stuff the poor man could expect to get for the first six months. It'll be pure routine to begin with.'

Outside the office, John's help proved invaluable. He helped her sell her car, find a new tenant for her flat, despatch the unexpected number of crates into which she packed her books and valuables, and squired her through the succession of farewell parties that various colleagues held for her. Becky was grateful and at the same time a little guilty; she felt she was trespassing unfairly on his consideration by annexing so much of his time. On the other hand, she consoled herself, when she was permanently in England and he no longer saw her at all, he would forget soon enough.

She said as much to him one evening, when he had driven her home to her flat, an exercise he was increasingly called upon to perform now that she had disposed of her old Renault.

'Forget you? You don't overrate yourself, do you, Becky?'

'John, my dear, you and I have had nothing in common except propinquity. When that's removed, I'll fade gently out of your memory.'

'Yes?' he said politely. 'You are of course speaking from your own experience.'

She bit her lip. 'I asked for that.'

'You did,' he agreed. He leant across and opened the door for her, kissing her lightly. 'Goodnight, Becky. You sort out your own life and leave me to worry about mine.'

'But you've been so kind . . .'

'Pure self-indulgence,' he assured her, 'you mustn't imagine me to be a martyr or something stupid like that. I do what I want because I enjoy it—most people do. Never believe anyone who tells you he's sacrificing himself for somebody else. People do what they want to.'

She thought of Charles and his concern for Tessa. 'Not always,' she said wryly.

'Nonsense.' He looked at her quickly and judged it a good moment to tell her something he had been putting off for some days. 'For instance, I'm going back to London at the end of next week. The usual consultations, you know. I thought—if it would be useful—I could take the same flight as you do and help you with your baggage. Yes, I know you think you've packed and sent everything, but you'll be astounded at how much you have left to take with you. I've done enough moving to speak with authority. You'll have a mountain of stuff, believe me. I can give you a hand with it—I'll even let you share my baggage allowance,' he added generously.

Becky laughed. 'An offer I can't refuse,' she commented. 'Thank you, John, you really are much too kind to me.'

His smile twisted. 'That's my business. Goodnight, my dear.'

He drove away then, but, true to his word, he accompanied her on her final exodus.

On the flight Becky was preoccupied. She had only the briefest respite between landing in England and having to be prepared to leave again; Miss Smart had arranged for her to pick up Tessa from Almcote Manor the day after tomorrow and accompany her to London, where they would meet Charles at the airport.

'I've hardly time to get my washing done,' Becky complained to John Townsend, reviewing Miss Smart's arrangements. 'I suppose I shall have to rely on my mother to send things to the cleaners. It's a terrible nuisance. I virtually had to pack for the holiday in France.'

'Are you looking forward to it?' he asked curiously.

'I wasn't,' she admitted. 'Tessa has the reputation of being difficult, whatever that means. But I'm so tired, I can't think of a holiday with anything except vast relief.'

'And when do you get married?' he probed.

But that was too much. She began to fold up the little tray in front of her into the slot on the seat ahead with an attention that the simple operation surely did not warrant. Her lids veiled her eyes and her expression was quite blank. John, not for the first time that month, had the uncomfortable feeling that he was in the company of an incalculable stranger.

Becky had been grateful for his assistance, generous in acknowledging it, and, up to a point, unexpectedly frank. But John Townsend felt that an invisible line had been drawn beyond which he was not permitted to venture. Once or twice in conversation with her he had approached it, and felt Becky not withdraw, so much as prepare to resist intrusion. As she was doing now.

He sighed. 'Don't forget my invitation to the wedding, anyway.'

She chuckled. 'Certainly not! If anyone ever earned his free champagne, it's you.'

'Yes,' he agreed wryly.

When they were finally released by the Customs officers, who had displayed a benevolent but baffled interest in Becky's assorted impedimenta, John accompanied her into the main lounge. It was full of friends and relations meeting passengers, and he raised an enquiring eyebrow at her.

'Do you want a lift in my taxi to London, or are you being met?'

Becky shook her head. 'I can't face fighting through the crowds at Paddington with all my boxes. I'll hire a car. There are usually plenty available and I can take it into Swindon to leave it. Nobody is meeting me.'

'Then I'll say goodbye.' He surrendered the baggage trolley he had been pushing, hesitated, took a step towards her and then swept her a little desperately into his arms. Becky was touched.

'Goodbye, John,' she said gently as he released her.

She stood looking after him as he strode off through the crush, her eyes glistening with tears, for John and herself, and for the life she had so decisively quitted. A hand with a snowy handkerchief appeared at her elbow.

'Have a good blow,' said a not unkindly voice in her ear.

She turned, her heart thumping, to find Charles looking down at her.

'What—what are you doing here?' she managed.

'Making a rather inefficient job of meeting you,' he said literally. He looked at his watch. 'The trouble is that my timetable is a bit tight. I've got to be off to Aberdeen in half an hour, but it occurred to me that you could do with a hand with your luggage. Obviously Townsend had the same idea.'

To her fury Becky blushed, and Charles surveyed the phenomenon thoughtfully. 'He's been very good,' she said.

The corner of Charles' mouth twitched. 'Yes? Well, he probably felt he owed it to you. You've towed him out of enough deep water in your time. He was probably in despair at saying goodbye. It's to be hoped that his next assistant proves an equally efficient prop.'

'Don't!' exclaimed Becky involuntarily.

116

'Perhaps I'm not entirely fair about him,' Charles admitted. 'At least I should be grateful that he gave you a hand with your paraphernalia. Look, you'd better have these.' He handed her two keys on a leather ring. 'The car's in the car park—Annabella wrote the number of the parking bay on the ticket.' He fished that out of his pocket and handed that to her as well. 'Oh, and she's put the registration number on it as well. It's a dark green Porsche. You should find it fairly easily. It's on the third level, as far as I remember.'

'Thank you,' said Becky, nonplussed.

'I thought that if you were going to chauffeur my sister up to London the least I could do was provide the transport,' he said charmingly. He looked over her head. 'Ah, there's Annabella. They must have called our flight. She told me she'd come and find me when they did.'

'I see.' Becky stood a little helplessly, swinging the keys, as a dark striking-looking woman threaded her way through the jostling throng towards them.

Becky's eyes widened. She had been prepared by Charles for something special in the way of secretaries, but Miss Smart was spectacular. In fact, mused Becky, thinking of her own dear Janet Hardy, she hardly resembled any member of that species that she had ever encountered before. They were introduced.

Clearly the lady was much attached to Charles, and equally clearly he was aware of it. There was a certain rueful familiarity in his manner to her which suggested they were intimates. Almost, mused Becky, finding she disliked the idea, conspirators. Miss Smart was pleasant but guarded, and Becky didn't quite know how to respond. She recognised with unerring instinct that in Annabella Smart she beheld the kind of beauty and style to attract Charles—she was of the same type as the several other exotic ladies that Becky had from time to time encountered in his company: cool, with a hint of hidden ferocity, exquisitely turned out, clever. The sort of woman, she acknowledged ruefully, just calculated to fill her with a sense of her own imperfections, particularly after a gruelling journey.

Soon enough Miss Smart drew Charles away, murmuring that they had only twenty minutes to board their plane.

'Yes, all right,' said Charles impatiently. He kissed Becky briefly on the cheek. 'Oh, there's something for you in the car,' he added as an afterthought.

Annabella smiled at her, though her eyes remained cold. 'I hope you like it,' she said in her soft voice, 'they're very fashionable just now. If you'd rather have another colour you must let me know and I can change it easily enough.'

Becky was utterly taken aback.

Charles looked from one woman to the other with a look of secret and intense amusement on his face.

'Efficient Annabella,' he remarked.

It was a shawl, soft as silk and a lovely watery moonlight colour. Becky would have loved it, had it not been for Annabella's involvement. Anyway, it served to impress not only her own family but the Mallorys. Judith in particular could not imagine a man bestowing an obviously expensive shawl upon a woman unless compelled thereto by affection or marital obligation. And, as she pointed out to Tessa, Charles and Becky weren't married yet.

The token greatly encouraged Tessa. She had been shocked by her mother's suggestion that Charles had the same casual opinion of marriage that she had herself, and consequently recoiled from Becky, but now she came to the conclusion that Judith was wrong and began to accept Becky's overtures of friendship in a more receptive spirit. She was very quiet, and Becky suspected that she had been somewhat chastened during her recent examinations, but she was friendly enough, and when they finally met Charles at the airport they were in very reasonable amity with each other.

CHAPTER SIX

The journey was an extended one: a late night flight to Istanbul followed, almost as soon as they landed, by a trip on an island-hopping ten-seater in the cool Aegean morning. They eventually landed on what appeared to be their eventual destination at eight o'clock.

Tessa, who had kept up an unending commentary on the islands below them, leaped out of the little plane before Charles or Becky had unbuckled their seat-belts. While Charles helped the pilot unload their cases Tessa danced off down what appeared to be a goat track.

'Tessa wants her breakfast,' observed Charles tolerantly, helping Becky out of the plane.

She looked about her. 'So do I,' she told him. 'Where are we?'

'Stranded on a desert island,' he said airily, 'at least until next Sunday when Janos comes back.'

He slammed the door of the plane and raised a friendly hand to the pilot before taking Becky's hand and urging her out of the vicinity of the makeshift runway.

Becky considered the prospect of a deserted island and found it restful. 'Good,' she said, as soon as the plane had taken off and she could hear herself speak. 'Do we pitch a tent, or do you think it worth while building a palm tree hut for a fortnight?'

He chuckled. 'No, on balance I don't think I want to do anything as energetic as building a cabin. Especially as there's a perfectly good house down there through the trees.'

She followed his gesture. They were on a central ridge which, from the air, had seemed to form the spine of the island. Now she could see that where the slopes fell away from this plateau there were pines and olive trees. Somewhere in the middle of them she thought she could make out a gleam of white which she took to be the house.

'So it's not a desert island after all,' she said, disappointed.

He laughed, picking up one of their cases. 'Well, it's got running water and the house has a generator that sometimes works. And there's a couple that looks after the house and another family that farms the olive groves. Half a dozen goats and a couple of donkeys and you have a full run-down on the indigenous population.' He offered her his free hand and began to pull her down a rough but clearly marked track. 'Come and meet them. No doubt they heard the plane and Tessa's probably already tucking into bread and honey.'

Becky followed, half laughing, half protesting.

'What about the cases?' she reminded him. 'Shouldn't I bring one?'

'I'll come and collect them with the donkeys later,' he assured her. 'In the meantime they'll be quite safe. We don't have thieves on the island and it will hardly rain.'

She scanned the blue horizon appreciatively. 'No indeed, it's already warm.'

'Wait until midday,' he warned. 'Then it's so warm you have to run across the sand to the water or you burn your feet.'

'Sounds enticing.' She leant backwards trying to break his headlong speed down the steep path. 'No, Charles, please wait a bit. I want to take off my blazer—I'm boiling!'

He paused obediently, dropping her wrist. 'Just leave it on the ground,' he told her, 'I'll fetch it when I come for the cases.'

She divested herself of the coat. 'You really don't have thieves, then?'

He grinned like a schoolboy. 'None that would be tempted by couturier clothes! A packet of jam sandwiches, now, and the story might be different'

Becky untied the scarf round her throat and rolled the sleeves of her silk shirt up above her elbows. 'How heavenly!' She stretched her arms above her head in a sudden excess of satisfaction with the day and the landscape.

Charles looked up at her, his eyes half closed against the glare of the sun. 'I'm gratified.'

'Because I like it here?' She stared at him. 'But who wouldn't?'

'More than half the world. The vast majority of my acquaintance. There isn't anything to do, you know, unless you fancy picking a few early olives.'

'Do I? I don't intend to do anything. I'm going to take a leaf out of your book and sleep in the sun all day.'

'Very companionable,' he commented. 'Are you going to stand there waving your arms at the sun all day, or can we get down to the house and have some breakfast?'

'Oh!' She jumped guiltily. 'I'm sorry, I didn't think.' She scrambled down the few steps to join him and slipped her hand in the crook of his arm. 'It's all so perfect. How on earth did you find it?'

'I've been here before,' he said evasively, changing the suitcase to his other hand.

Contrite, she dropped his arm. 'Oh, I'm sorry, I forgot you were carrying that. Anyway, why are you? What's in it that's so precious it can't be left to be collected by the donkeys?'

'One or two essentials I thought we might need immediately.'

Becky was intrigued. 'What do you consider essentials?'

'Swimsuits, snorkels and a packet of coffee,' he said fluently.

'*Coffee?*'

'I've been here before,' he said again. 'Come *on*, Becky.'

She went with him thoughtfully. It occurred to her that she had not seen him looking so young and carefree before; even as a boy he had always had a certain sardonic element in even his best humour. She had never before seen him so unguardedly happy. He must, she deduced, like his island very much. Probably it had happier memories than Almcote Manor.

They came out of the trees on to a dusty patio where a dark smiling woman awaited them.

'Welcome back, Mr Charles,' she said. 'We heard the plane and Stathis pumped the water in case you want a shower. Breakfast is ready when you want it.'

'Oh, excellent, Elena,' he said, dumping the case with a flurry of dust and kissing her heartily on both cheeks. 'I do indeed want a shower. And so, I imagine, does Becky. Oh, by the way, this is Becky, Elena. The small tornado that you have no doubt already encountered was my little sister.'

Elena inclined her head to Becky. 'Good morning, Miss Becky. Mr Charles wrote and told us that you were coming.' She looked a little anxious. 'I hope you will not be uncomfortable.'

'I'm sure I won't,' said Becky, startled, one eyebrow raised enquiringly at Charles.

'Some of our earlier guests have found it a trifle Spartan,' he explained, and began to rummage in the case he had brought with him. At length he triumphantly raised a four-ounce tin of coffee above his head. 'There we are. When you've brewed that, Elena my love, I for one shall be very ready for breakfast. If you go now,' he added to Becky, 'you can have the shower first. Otherwise I shall yield to my baser instincts and grab it.'

Elena looked a little shocked, but Becky laughed. 'How chivalrous! I can hardly refuse.'

As she made her way into the dark interior, she met Tessa.

'Isn't it super?' exclaimed Tessa, all hostility left behind in London. 'I've got a room in the tower above the kitchen and I can see the coast of the mainland. And we've got our own beach. But Stathis says no one ever goes on any of the beaches here because there aren't any hotels, so we might just as well have the whole island to ourselves. *And* there are donkeys—Stathis says I can ride one up the hill to collect the luggage if I like. Oh, I do want to explore!'

'I'm sure you do,' agreed Becky, a little amused. 'Er—on a donkey?'

'If Stathis will let me,' replied Tessa serenely. 'Are you ready for breakfast? I'm so hungry!'

'I'll be as quick as I can,' promised Becky.

In fact she saw very little of Tessa for the rest of the day. By the time she and Charles appeared for breakfast Tessa, deciding that freshly-pressed orange juice made an infinitely preferable substitute for percolated coffee, had finished eating and departed with Stathis and his animals. On her return she acknowledged them briefly, then dozing over the last of the coffee, before bustling off with the avowed intention of circumnavigating the island on a donkey.

Becky was surprised that Charles did not object to Tessa courting sunstroke by taking violent exercise as soon as she had eaten, but Charles merely raised a negligent hand in farewell and reminded her to wear a hat.

Charles, again to her surprise, revelled in the heat. As soon as he could he escaped to the beach; there was an impressive paved way from the house down to the beach, and he ran lightly from shallow sloping slab to slab. Elena watched him approvingly.

'He always does that,' she told Becky smilingly, confirming her suspicion that he was a familiar visitor to the island.

'It's a wonder he doesn't break his neck,' said Becky in some anxiety, 'those stones look dreadfully uneven. Couldn't something be done about them?'

Elena was torn between shock and amusement. 'They are very old. They were here before the villa. There used to be a temple on the island and nobody lived here but the priests; the people used to bring gifts up that path and leave them outside the temple. Of course, when the Turks came the temple was deserted and in time it fell down, so only the causeway remains now. But I do not think it would be easy to get permission to mend the steps. They are the only antiquity on the island.'

'I see,' said Becky, chastened. A thought occurred to her. 'Do you mean that this house stands on the site of the temple?'

Elena shook her head. 'Oh no. It was on the top of the hill, so that it could be seen for miles. It was a landmark to sailors. The villa is only halfway up the causeway; it goes on up the hill behind the villa.' She gestured with her hand. 'There, round the headland. Mr Charles will take you up there. It is very beautiful and we often take picnics there, but the causeway gets worse and it is very steep.'

'I'll remember,' murmured Becky, narrowing her eyes to look at the imposing skyline that Elena indicated. It lowered over the house almost threateningly, dark with the inevitable pines. She gave a little shiver in spite of the blinding heat on the patio and looked longingly down at the beach spread below her.

Charles was now a tiny figure, almost disappearing as he flung himself into the sea and struck out strongly.

'Do you want to swim, Miss Becky? I have unpacked the case Mr Charles brought down with you. There is a beach towel in your bathroom.'

Becky smiled. 'Thank you, Elena.' Bowing to the inevitable, she did as she felt she had been instructed to do, changed quickly and made her way down to the beach in Charles' wake, albeit at a rather more moderate pace.

Once there, she swam briefly and, as Charles was out of sight, settled down in the sun and dozed off. A couple of times she roused herself enough to apply sun lotion to her unaccustomed skin. Once Charles was there, on his back with his eyes closed. He opened one eye and smiled at her as she moved. She smiled back, too lazy to speak, and was soon asleep again.

The day was a long one and Charles a relaxed, obliging companion. Elena sent down her son with an enormous hamper of food, most of which Becky and Charles fed to the gulls. Bewildered by this unexpected largesse, the birds sat on the rocks of the headland and watched them with deep suspicion.

'They're beautiful,' said Becky dreamily. 'Are they rare?'

'The gulls? I shouldn't think so. There's always been a singularly rapacious colony of them here, anyway.'

'They're not rapacious,' she objected, 'they're only taking what I give them.'

'Ah yes, but you've given them everything, haven't you?' said Charles, and she had the oddest feeling he wasn't talking about the gulls at all. 'Obviously they aren't going to dive-bomb an empty picnic basket.'

'You're probably right,' she agreed pacifically. 'Tell me, have you been here often?'

'Since I was a boy, on and off.'

'Really? I didn't know.'

'Why should you?' he said coolly. 'You don't know everything there is to be known about me, you know.'

'I'm beginning to realise that,' said Becky ruefully.

'Well, thank God for that at least!'

She didn't understand him and so had no idea how to answer. After a pause she said, 'It doesn't belong to your father, does it?'

'The island? Lord, no, it's my godfather's. I've always had the run of it.'

'Nice,' she commented.

'I think so, certainly.' He sat cross-legged, looking down at her. 'I wasn't altogether sure that you would, though.'

'Me? Why on earth not?'

'You're such a contradictory bundle of tastes and prejudices.'

Becky frowned. 'I don't believe that.'

'I suppose you wouldn't, but it's true nonetheless. With most people—most women—one knows more or less what will please them, what will hurt, to what they'll be indifferent. But you're never the same two days together. I never know which way you'll jump.'

She was troubled. 'But why, Charles? I mean, I've always been very ordinary.'

'Defiantly ordinary,' he said ironically.

'What do you mean?'

He sighed. 'Well, how many girls leave university and go back home to mother, never wanting to leave the nest again,' he countered. 'How many girls want to be country solicitors for the rest of their lives at twenty-two?'

'Quite a few, I should think,' she said calmly. 'Perhaps you just haven't met many others. But I shouldn't think home-loving creatures are too thin on the ground.'

'No, they're not, but home-loving creatures don't

normally push off into the wide blue yonder in a fit of pique, never to be heard of again.'

Becky jack-knifed upright as if he had hit her.

'It was not,' she said between her teeth, 'a fit of pique.'

'No? Then what was it? An undying love for Tony Boyd?'

'You,' crushingly, 'wouldn't understand.'

'Perhaps not, but you can try me.'

'No!' she gasped, in a panic-stricken reflex. 'No, I don't want to.'

He shrugged. 'As you please.'

Thoroughly unsettled, she stood up and walked away from him down the deserted beach. He made no attempt to follow her and after a few minutes, he stood up and plunged back into the sea.

Becky walked on. She had expected Charles to bring up the subject of her previous engagement earlier, and when he did not do so she had assumed that he would continue to ignore the subject. After all, it was a long time ago and he must have imagined that she would have recovered by now. Undoubtedly that was what her family thought. Nobody stayed faithful to the memory of a man who, having tried his best to cheat her family, showed no repentance and, within a year of having his ring returned, married someone else. No, she mused, kicking up sand and running it warmly through her toes, not so much as a year; a few months only. He must already have been seeing her before Becky left England.

She sank down on a rock, putting a surprised family of gulls to flight. She didn't notice.

Yes, it had undoubtedly all been very lowering. Holed up in Strasbourg, she had bandaged her pride with work and more work. In her efforts to banish Tony from her mind she had driven herself to the point of collapse. Tired, humiliated and bitterly lonely in the foreign city, she had vowed that she would never again put her happiness in hazard. Some of this she had tried to convey to John Townsend, without much success. Now it looked as if she were going to have to explain it to Charles after all, when she had decided that he wasn't in the least interested.

He emerged from the sea at her feet, his hair wet as a seal's. 'Hullo,' he said tranquilly, shaking the water from his eyes. 'Exploring, or just taking a constitutional?'

She looked at her bare feet ruefully. 'I'm not dressed for exploring. Those rocks look tough.'

'Softy,' he mocked.

'It's all very well for you, you've been here since you were a child and know what to expect. I'd want some shoes with decent soles to them before I go scrambling on those great heaps of stone. I hope you brought some.'

He looked struck. 'I never thought of it, unless Annabella put some in on her own initiative.'

'Annabella?'

'Yes, Annabella Smart. You met her the day before yesterday, if you remember. She did my last-minute shopping in Aberdeen.'

'Oh,' said Becky, her pleasure in the place inexplicably dimmed. 'Oh yes, of course.'

'She might have done so, of course,' he pondered, pursuing his own train of thought. 'She's been here, which is one of the reasons I enlisted her aid. I don't remember whether we scaled those cliffs, though. Probably not.'

Becky thought. 'Was she the guest that found it all too —what was your word?—Spartan?'

His eyes lifted quickly. 'Ten out of ten for deduction. Yes, I wouldn't dare bring Annabella here again. She complained for weeks, and I nearly lost her. Good lord, of course she didn't climb those cliffs. She was rude enough about the causeway to the beach.'

'I see,' said Becky with admirable calm. 'Well, unless she decided that I was made of different mettle and put in some good stout shoes, I'm not going up there either. Not in bare feet.'

He chuckled. 'It amazes me that you'd contemplate going up there at all. It's not a climb for the timid.'

Becky gave him a measuring look. 'Are you being insulting, Charles?'

'Trying, merely trying.'

She laughed at his ingenuous expression. 'Why?'

'Because you're much more fun when you're in a flaming temper,' he told her. 'Still, you're clearly not going to retaliate on an empty stomach. Let's go and see what Elena's concocted for us.'

They toiled back up the hillside in companionable silence. Apart from Tessa's tower, the house was long and only a single storey high. The ceilings were immensely lofty and the floors were of an echoing marble which Elena had polished so diligently that they reflected the inhabitants of the house like dark ghosts. At first it struck Becky as rather a gloomy place, but she soon found that the contrived cool was a blessed sanctuary from the outdoors.

When they came in sight of the house Elena was to be seen on the patio, setting plates on the iron table that stood in the lee of the kitchen wall. As they got closer they saw that she was only laying two places. 'Tessa's obviously not back,' observed Charles. 'Probably asleep under an olive tree somewhere.' He grinned. 'Those wooden donkey saddles can be tough riding.'

Becky looked reproving. 'In that case we shall have to go and find her.'

He shrugged. 'Oh, nonsense, she won't come to any harm. And there's a ton of embrocation in the first aid cupboard for when she does finally make it.'

When questioned, Elena volunteered only that Tessa was tired and had gone to bed as soon as she returned.

'Ah, those saddles!' sighed Charles.

'I'll go and see how she is,' said Becky hastily, feeling that Tessa would get less than the sympathy due to her from her brother.

'Do,' Charles urged her cordially. 'But don't be late for dinner.'

As it turned out Tessa was stiff but not badly overtired, and quite determined to talk about the discoveries of her day, so that Becky did not escape for some time. Then she luxuriated in a bath to rid herself of the specks of sand and smell of seaweed that had accumulated during the day.

It was therefore rather more than an hour later when she made her way back to the patio to find that Elena had prepared a perfect supper of fish with a salad of sliced tomatoes and black olives. The wine was chilled and resinated in a stone bottle from which the ice was melting in huge drops. Becky was surprised to discover that although there was a faint breeze redolent of the sea, the air was almost as warm as by day.

By the time she joined Charles it was nearly dark, and he and Elena were squabbling over an oil lamp. Pausing in the doorway, Becky watched in some amazement. Charles was of the opinion that as she had taken so long to change they would be eating in virtual darkness, they needed oil lamps to guide their knives and forks. With this argument, however, the romantic Elena would by no means agree.

'But no, Mr Charles,' she was insisting. 'If you put a light in the middle of the table it will draw insects. Miss Becky will be bitten by midges.'

'She should have thought of that before she retired to the bathroom for the evening,' said Charles unchivalrously, but with pardonable exaggeration.

'I know,' said Becky, intervening as she came forward. 'I'm very sorry, I lost count of time. Are you dreadfully hungry?'

He looked up and his eyes met hers, filled with laughter. 'Dreadfully.'

'Then I'm truly sorry. I'll eat under a spotlight to atone, if you like.'

'No, Elena's right. You'd get bitten to pieces.'

Satisfied, Elena whisked the oil lamp out of his grasp before he could change his mind, and retreated to the house.

'It would probably have exploded anyway,' said Charles philosophically. 'I have a nasty habit of turning the lighted wick down into the oil and setting off a big bang. There must be an incendiarist in my family tree.'

'In that case, I'm more than ever glad Elena took it away.'

He chuckled. 'It wouldn't have been an auspicious way to start a marriage, I agree.'

He brought her a glass of wine.

'It wouldn't,' she agreed composedly, accepting it. 'Anyway, it's not all that dark.' She walked to the edge of the patio. 'The stars are incredible—I've never seen them like that before except at the Planetarium.' She broke off, finding that he was roaring with laughter. Suspecting an insult, she put up her brows. 'Explain the witticism.'

'You,' he said succinctly. 'You are constant delight. Do you know how many girls have stood there, saying "Ah, the moon, ah, the stars"? And not one of them has ever said it was as good as the Planetarium before.'

Becky chuckled. 'I may have been a little prosaic,' she allowed.

'A spot lacking in poetry,' he agreed, 'but wholly characteristic.' He perched negligently on the low white wall that ran round the patio. 'You're hardly a romantic, are you, Becky?'

'No, no more than you are,' she pointed out.

'Ah, but you don't know me very well.' His voice was wickedly amused.

'Are you trying to tell me you *are* romantic?' she demanded incredulously.

He put his head on one side. 'It depends what you mean by romantic. Possibly not by your standards—if I loved someone I wouldn't run away and disappear into oblivion. I'd stick around and wait—do something if I could, and if I couldn't, just wait.'

Almost imperceptibly she drew back, her hands clenching round the goblet he had given her. 'Now you're back to Tony. Out with it, Charles. What do you want to know?'

He said gently, 'Nothing you don't want to tell me.'

'I——' She bit it off and swung away from him.

Looking at her averted profile, he told her, 'If you want to take the opportunity to lay the ghost, carry on. Otherwise forget it. It's none of my business after all.'

Ironically, now that he had disavowed any inclination to hear, she wanted to tell him. Wondering at her own contrariness, Becky said slowly, 'It was all my pride. That's why I'm so touchy, I suppose. I'd gambled it all on Tony.'

'Your *pride*?'

'Yes. You see, nobody liked him—Aunt Edith said he was an upstart. Well, she would.'

'And you went on a crusade on his behalf?' He sighed. 'Well, it's predictable.'

'Oh no! I was in love with him. The full works. I lived from phone call to phone call. It had never happened to me before, and I couldn't disguise it. I wouldn't have known how to.'

'I remember,' he said.

'Yes, you would, of course. It was all so public.'

'So what happened?' he prompted. 'Did he walk out on you for the Shepherd girl?'

Becky had drifted into the bad memories, and came out of them with a start. 'Oh no, at least not that I was aware of. I didn't even know of her existence. No, it was nastier than that. He worked for Aunt Edith, and apparently he'd been less than honest. I don't understand it all, to be truthful. I was so overwrought I didn't take much notice of the details.'

'What details?' he asked as she trailed off unhappily.

'He was a thief,' she said distastefully, 'he'd been cooking the books for weeks. Apparently he had made off with jewellery as well, though I don't think he'd touched any of Aunt Edith's stuff; I never really gathered. The thing was that Aunt Edith had proof. She'd always hated our engagement, and she said she'd not go to the police if I broke it off.'

Her shoulders were rigid as if to sustain remembered pain, and she put the goblet down in front of her, very carefully, on the white stone wall. Aunt Edith's malevolent face rose before her and she closed her eyes.

'I told her I wouldn't be blackmailed,' she said proudly. 'Oh, I was shocked, of course, and hurt, but I could understand him doing it. He'd had so little all his life and all his friends in Almcote were rich—well, even we were, by his standards—and they were all so snobbish to him. It was revenge on them as much as greed. I'd not have thrown him over.'

Behind her Charles made a violent movement, quickly suppressed as she looked round.

'When you love someone,' she said, as she had never had the opportunity to say to Tony Boyd, 'you don't love them piecemeal. You don't say, I'll take all their good qualities, everything that makes them entertaining, and then abandon them when they do something you don't like.'

'So how did Aunt Edith persuade you to abandon Boyd?'

She laughed harshly. 'Oh, he did that for himself. He didn't want to go to prison, so he pointed out at length how extremely uncomfortable it would be for both of us.'

'So you broke the engagement and he married Megan Shepherd.'

'As you say,' she agreed.

'And you wasted two years of your life on the creature.'

There was a faint glimmer of a smile for that. 'Not wasted. I had a very rewarding career.'

'I hope you did.' He sighed impatiently. 'Oh, Becky, you're so busy taking care of other people you've never properly learnt to look after yourself.'

'Oh, that's not true,' she protested. 'It might have been two years ago, but I've grown up a bit since then.'

'Have you?' he said wryly. 'Throwing yourself into the breach when your mama lost her shirt? Holding the clown Townsend's hand every time he had to present a report? Marrying me as you were prepared to? Becky, have you *any* idea how dangerous it is to marry somebody when you're still in love with someone else? Because you are, aren't you? I thought you'd got some maternal fixation on Townsend, but I was wrong. You're still in love with Tony Boyd.'

'No!' her instinctive rejection of the idea was impassioned. 'No, I'm not. I'm not in love with anybody.'

CHAPTER SEVEN

HE would have said more, but Elena appeared with a steaming pot of what proved to be chicken soup and they were compelled by her benevolent eye to sit down to their meal.

Charles recovered his poise easily and chatted with Elena as she served that and the succeeding courses. Becky found it harder and was almost silent, although she managed to compliment Elena on the delicious food. At last Elena brought out a tray with two squat little cups on it and a burnished copper pot of coffee, and said goodnight.

'I hope you like Turkish coffee,' Charles said lightly. 'I do myself, though I draw the line at taking it for breakfast, which is why I always bring my own supply whenever I visit.'

'I—why yes, I think so. I haven't had it very often.'

He poured her a cup and handed it to her. 'I hope it's sweet enough. You put the sugar in while you're brewing, and I don't care for too much. Elena and Stathis drink it like molasses with a faint coffee flavour. They also make it with rosewater, which scents it. While I'm here they bow to my foreign prejudices, but I'm sure if you want it sweet and scented Elena will be delighted to make it to your taste.'

'Thank you.' Becky supped experimentally. It was a thicker brew than that to which she was accustomed, but it had a pleasantly nutty flavour, accentuated by the sugar in it. 'It's nice. I don't normally take sugar at all.'

'You wouldn't like this without sugar,' he assured her,

'it's bitter. They must roast the beans very hard, or something. And don't drain it to the dregs—there's a pile of river sludge at the bottom of the cup, you'll find. You have to throw it away before you get a refill.'

'Thank you,' said Becky again, meekly.

He lit a cigarette and tilted his chair back against the wall, studying her. Convinced that he could see no more of her expression than she of his, she bore his scrutiny calmly. The cigarette glowed red as he drew a luxurious lungful of smoke.

Idly she asked, 'Do you smoke a great deal?'

'Sometimes. When I'm tired, when I'm worried, when I have to concentrate ... It's purely psychological. I can go for weeks without touching a cigarette.'

'And what are you now?'

'I don't follow.'

'Tired, worried or concentrating?' she reminded him.

'A little of all three, I suppose.' The cigarette glowed again once or twice, and then he said abruptly out of the darkness, 'I meant what I was saying earlier, you know. I didn't believe you were still so committed to Boyd,' he added, with apparent irrelevance.

'I've told you, I'm not,' she snapped. 'And if I were it wouldn't make any difference. You know we agreed that this was an ordinary commercial contract. And temporary.'

'Yes, we did, didn't we?' he said wryly.

'Having second thoughts?' she mocked.

'It's a bit late for that.' He was unusually sober. 'Or is it? Do you want to back out?'

'Default on a contract?' Her humour restored, Becky was cheerfully teasing him. 'Really, Charles! What do you think I am?'

Unexpectedly she got a literal answer. 'A fool,' he said resoundingly, standing up so abruptly that his chair crashed over behind him. 'A blind, obstinate, wilful fool.'

'Maybe,' said Becky, declining to retort in kind, 'but I keep my promises.'

'Oh lord, yes, you do.' The resignation in his voice would have been almost comical if Becky had not sensed behind it some dark anger at whose source she could not make the remotest guess. She shuddered.

'Are you cold?' he said at once, revealing how little his eyes missed.

'Not particularly.'

'There's a breeze—have you got a coat?'

'I left a shawl in the bedroom.' A lovely lacy thing she would have instantly taken to her heart if only it had not been bought for her by the ubiquitous Miss Smart. 'It's on the chair.'

'I'll get it.'

When he was gone she walked to the low parapet and stood staring out at the sea. In the distance she could see three small lights, presumably belonging to vessels. The light wind that fanned her cheek had definitely cooled since they sat down to eat and she wondered how late it was. Clasping her arms about her, she listened to the soft hushing of the water against the rocks below the house. It was very peaceful; in spite of the rather strained atmosphere with Charles, she was enjoying this place.

She did not hear his step behind her, so intent was she on her own thoughts, until he dropped the shawl about her.

'You *are* cold.'

'A little,' she acknowledged, surprised at his concern and shaken off balance by it, 'not unduly. There's no need to make an accusation of it, I shan't die of a little cold.'

He drew a sharp breath and his hands closed on her elbows drawing her back against him.

'No, by God,' he said, 'but I might.'

He put his lips to her temple. Against her will, obeying an instinct she had never before discovered, Becky's head went back. Somewhere, faintly, a voice mocked her. This is stupidity, it said; this isn't your lover or even a friend. This is Charles, smooth clever Charles, who finds out what he wants from people and then turns it against them. She ignored it. Trembling but passive, she leant against him. His heart was thudding like a runner's, and she could feel it against her shoulder blade. His mouth moved murmurously on her soft skin; almost inaudibly he was saying her name over and over again. Then, with ravishing gentleness, he put the shawl and the strap of her dress away from her shoulder and kissed it. Becky caught fire.

It was unexpected; it was highly unlikely: it was the most disastrous possible outcome of what had always threatened to be an unsafe enterprise. But for a few tumultuous seconds Becky was beyond reflection. Once bridged, her defences were, she found, paltry things. They not so much crumbled as vanished as if at an enchanter's spell.

Only when the shawl entangled with her hair, fell away from her, was she recalled to herself. Gathering it about her with shaking fingers, she drew back. Its warmth was comforting, and she wondered, for a fiercely painful moment, if Annabella Smart had bought it with just such an evening in mind. Reminded that his only gift to her had been of Annabella's choosing, she discovered that it would be quite easy to hate Charles if she put her mind to it.

'Becky ...' he began.

'Don't!' Her voice was barely recognisable. Shaking pitiably, she managed, 'I don't know why you did that, Charles, but please don't again. I can't bear the—the *pretence*.'

'What pretence?' he murmured, drawing her back into his arms.

'This ...' Who would have believed that Charles, her ancient enemy, could move her so sweetly? His touch was a challenge and a delight. In something like panic she cried out to him, 'It's only second best. It won't do! Can't you see that it won't do?'

As if she had struck him, he recoiled.

Becky pulled Annabella's shawl about her suddenly hunched shoulders.

'I'd forgotten it was second best,' he said, heavily ironic, 'just for the moment, you understand. And so had you.'

She gasped. 'That's not ...'

'Not what? Kind? Chivalrous?'

'Both.'

'Oh, agreed, but then I never pretended I was either of those estimable things. You knew that when you agreed to come. You've known it all your life.'

Becky gathered the tatters of her dignity about her. 'I didn't know you'd go so far just to—just to get the better of me,' she said quietly.

Charles drew a weary hand through his wildly disordered hair. 'Oh, Becky, you're living in a dream world,' he said.

'Because I don't want to pretend?'

'Because you don't want to wake up,' he said brutally. 'You're old enough to face facts. Look at it—two years ago you made a bad mistake. Not a fatal one, but bad enough. Well, I'm sorry, but it's over now. Put it behind you.' He shook her, not gently. 'Boyd didn't want you.'

She flinched in his hands, but he was quite unrelenting. 'He didn't and you know it. It's about time you started noticing that there are other people who do.'

'Like you?' she queried savagely.

'Precisely.'

'Among how many others, Charles?'

'Oh, you're impossible!' He almost flung her away from him.

Hurt, and horrified at the extent of it, she was as insulting as she could be.

'This may be a commercial contract, this engagement of ours, Charles, but you can't *buy* from me what I gave Tony,' she flung at him.

'What makes you think I would want it?' He was quite as angry as she but, as always, he kept a cooler head. 'You're hysterical. Go and put your head under the shower or something. I'm going for a walk, and when you've had your little fit of hysteria perhaps we can talk as sensible human beings again.'

He swung off into the shadows.

She heard his shoes on the uneven steps. Even in the midst of her fury she remembered the quality of those steps, and ran anxiously to the parapet to see whether he was all right. But his steps faded into the silence and she assumed he would make his way safely to the beach. After all, he knew the path.

A little shakily, she sat down on the wall. Charles had left his cigarettes on the table among the remains of their meal, and she helped herself to one before she discovered that he had taken his lighter with him. Petulantly she pitched it over the wall.

Almost at once she heard a thin, wailing cry, hardly human, a long-drawn-out shriek of terror and pain that brought hairs on the back of her neck up on end. Her heart helt as if it stopped beating.

'Oh, my God,' she said out loud, '*Charles!*'

With some confused idea that her cigarette had caught him by surprise and somehow toppled him down those treacherous steps, she fled after him. There was a pain, like a great weight, in her lungs and she missed her footing several times, but she was all right until she came to the first curve in the pilgrim's causeway. Then, turning her ankle on a particularly steep stair, she tripped, staggered, almost recovered her balance and lost it finally with despairing abandon. The last thing she remembered was hurtling, head first, down that stone ramp to the beach, calling on Charles.

It was there that he found her, sticky with blood from wounds that in the dark he could only guess at. Fearing to move her and equally fearing to leave her exposed to the treacherous early morning air, he decided, in the end, that the only thing was to take her back to the villa.

When he lifted her, she turned her head fretfully from side to side, whimpering. It was a chilling sound, the more so because he knew she would never have permitted herself to make it if she had been conscious.

Very, very gently he began to climb the hill, the gulls wheeling and screaming above his head, the girl in his arms, as it seemed to him, barely breathing.

CHAPTER EIGHT

As soon as was practicable in the morning, Charles used the short-wave radio to call a doctor, who flew out from the mainland in a noisy little helicopter and pronounced Becky's injuries more gory than serious. He was a large, friendly man, clearly more interested in the villa and the island than the health of the eccentric foreign lady. When pressed by Charles, he admitted that without X-rays it was impossible to be wholly positive that Miss Summerson had not sustained any permanent injury.

But it was unlikely, he opined. She had broken her wrist, which he strapped up promptly, but otherwise, although badly grazed and shaken, she was perfectly well. The slight fever that had manifested itself was almost certainly due to shock. There was little danger of infection, although he good-humouredly gave Becky an anti-tetanus injection at Charles' insistence. At length he took his leave with some reluctance, consoled only by the prospect of the ride back to his surburban practice in Mr Mallory's specially-chartered helicopter.

Charles went to Becky, having seen him off. She was flushed and unhappy, and he stood looking down at her thoughtfully.

'How are you now?'

'Much better,' she said politely.

'No, you're not,' he contradicted calmly. 'I wish I was sure that old fool knew what he was doing. How's the head?'

'Protesting,' she admitted. 'It doesn't like being bounced downstairs.'

He smiled. 'And who shall blame it?' Frowning, he sat on the edge of the bed and put his cool hand against her brow. 'I'm not sure what to do—you've got a temperature. Try to sleep. If you don't feel any better when you wake up, we're going home.'

'Home?' Becky was startled. 'I thought we were marooned here until next Sunday.'

'Oh, regular transport!' He dismissed it with a shrug. 'I can charter a plane to take us back to Istanbul and then we ought not to have any trouble picking up an early plane for London.'

She was awed. 'But the expense——' she murmured faintly.

He gave her his sudden schoolboy grin. 'It wouldn't be nearly as expensive as a new head,' he assured her, getting up. 'Don't worry, see how you're feeling later.'

But later she was hot and querulous and in pain, although she did her best to disguise it. Elena was troubled and supported Charles in his swift decision to return to England. Not, as he told her, that there weren't plenty of excellent doctors in Istanbul, but if Becky was going to be ill it would be much better for her to be at home.

'With her family,' nodded kind Elena, and wondered at the sudden tightening of Charles' lips.

In the event, Becky's mother and sister descended upon London as soon as Charles told them the news. He whisked Becky back to England and into a nursing home with such expedition that, as she said afterwards, she hardly noticed it was happening. Nevertheless, Mrs Summerson was convinced that her daughter's accident was the result of some callous carelessness on his part. This distressed Becky, who was well aware that she owed her broken wrist to her own heedless folly, but Charles seemed to find it mildly amusing and made no attempt to defend himself against Mrs Summerson's veiled accusations.

She was in hospital for ten days, during which time Charles visited her with what she felt to be more duty than devotion. He was always kind—kinder, she felt, than she deserved—and he had a light touch which skilfully skirted the constraint between them. They never mentioned the quarrel which had preceded Becky's tumble down the hillside.

At first Becky was grateful for this forbearance, and then she began to chafe under the enforced silence it imposed on her. She discovered that she was compelled to meet his civility with composure which disguised her remorse and bewilderment. He gave her no opportunity to explain or even to apologise for her wild accusations that evening, and at least it was borne in upon her that he avoided the subject deliberately. Clearly for him the subject was closed permanently. Chilled, she retreated in her turn and took refuge in a remote friendliness which made her observant mother feel that all her worst predictions had been fulfilled.

Neither Charles nor Becky complained, however, and when Becky left hospital she returned composedly to the house that Charles had taken over from his father.

Charles had repeated his invitation to take over the top flat and Becky, with the prospect of numerous London interviews in the coming weeks, was happy enough to agree. Besides, she had something of a conscience about the way her accident had interrupted Tessa's holiday, and she registered a resolve to supply the deficiency during the summer holidays. Tessa had been philosophical —indeed she had been unwontedly quiet, a circumstance regarded with much suspicion by Mrs Summerson, who encountered her at Becky's bedside one afternoon.

'That girl is plotting something,' she told Becky when Tessa left.

'Who shall blame her?' said Becky. 'But I think you're wrong. I've asked Charles whether she can bring some friends back at the end of term—I mean, I shall hardly be installed in a job by that time and I could look after them, feed them and things. Charles need never see them.'

'And what did Charles say?'

Becky knit her brows. 'Oh, something oblique as he always does. It seemed to amuse him, but I don't think he'll object.'

'I'm sure he won't,' said her mother drily.

So Becky went back to the house wherein, amid painters, plumbers and plasterers, she applied for various jobs and spent a good deal of her time answering the telephone.

Almost at once Charles left for Europe; he had to go to Holland for consultations with a firm of advocates in Amsterdam, he told her. He was also worried about his father, and intended going on to Switzerland to visit him in his mountain fastness. Becky was rather relieved.

At first she was interested and discussed his proposed trip with him at some length. However, when he let fall that he was intending to take Annabella Smart with him as his personal assistant, she abruptly lost interest. Charles noted the reaction.

Feeling in need of physical activity, Becky threw herself into decorating one of the newly-painted rooms on the first floor against Tessa's eventual arrival. But the room housed an earlier occupant. Coming home from an enjoyable shopping expedition loaded with a decorative pile of dried grasses, Becky found that Judith Mallory, making use of her own door key, had installed herself in the absence of anyone to say her nay. Having barked her shins on Mrs Mallory's numerous suitcases, Becky found her upstairs.

'Hullo, Judith,' she said mildly. 'Setting off on a journey?'

Judith, who had been gazing rather disparagingly about the hastily-tidied bedroom, turned to face her, rather disconcerted.

'Coming to the end of one,' she corrected smoothly. She presented Becky with a softly powdered cheek. 'How are you, Becky? I'm glad to see you're better.' She inspected her narrowly. 'No permanent scars? Charles said you were a sight when he first brought you home.'

Becky laughed. 'I've still got some juicy scabs on my hip and my right leg if you're interested. I didn't scrape my face so badly, and the scars have gone.'

'How lucky,' observed Judith, managing to sound faintly malicious in expressing the charitable sentiment.

'Yes, isn't it?' Becky agreed. 'Are you staying long, Judith? I saw your cases in the hall.'

'Unless you won't have me,' said Mrs Mallory, opening enormous eyes to their fullest extent.

'Oh, but of course we'll have you,' Becky assured her with spurious amiability. 'It will be delightful, though I do hope you won't find yourself crowded.'

'Crowded?' repeated Judith, her eyes narrowing.

'By Tessa. Didn't she tell you? She's coming home here for the holidays, at least to begin with, and Charles did say that she could bring a friend if she wanted. Of course they'll have the big room on the first floor: it's still got two beds in it, but there's a load of other junk that we may have to store in here,' said Becky guilefully.

'Oh!' Judith looked discomposed. 'It doesn't sound as if I've picked my time very well, does it? But I thought, as Edward's wife, I have first priority in his house.'

'Charles' house,' said Becky gently.

'Well, yes, nominally . . .'

'Not nominally. In fact. Charles has taken over the deeds and Charles pays the bills.'

'It looks as if he's taken over my daughter as well!' snapped Judith, the civilised mask slipping.

'Not at all! If you don't want her to come and stay here, you have only to say so. I'm sure Charles will understand if you prefer to have her at home with you.'

There was a little silence while Judith glared at her antagonist.

'*Damn* you,' she said at last, with concentrated fury. 'This is your doing, you meddlesome creature.'

Becky raised her eyebrows. 'Charles' doing, surely?'

'Not without you to egg him on,' said Judith venomously. 'In fact, that's why he's marrying you, I'll bet.'

This was so near the truth that in spite of her resolution to ignore any of Judith Mallory's unpleasant sallies, Becky flinched. Judith saw it and instantly laughed.

'Not very good at hiding his intentions, Charles, is he? Did he warn you about Tessa?'

'*Warn* me? Certainly not, any more than I warned him about Chloe. We both knew what sort of family was included in the package.'

'I doubt it.' Judith laughed unkindly. 'So he didn't tell you that my delinquent daughter had contracted a nasty habit of running around with—er—undesirable characters? That in fact she's been drawn into the Shepherd circle? She actually brought Caradoc Shepherd to Almcote, did you know? Your mother and Charles climbed the curtains trying to keep it from you.'

Becky frowned. 'Caradoc Shepherd? The boy who has a sister at school with Tess? That hardly qualifies him as an undesirable character.'

'Don't be so stupid,' snapped Judith, losing patience, 'Caradoc's not a boy, he's over thirty, and anyway, he's more stupid than undesirable. It's his brother-in-law I object to.'

Becky looked puzzled and Judith began to laugh, a low, grating sound that alarmed her.

'You don't know, do you?' she said. 'Oh, this is priceless! Charles didn't even tell you. You don't know who it is Tessa's started to play with.'

'I don't see that it's any of my business,' said Becky, pretending an indifference she didn't feel. Judith's look of predatory satisfaction filled her with foreboding.

'Oh, but it is! Charles should have told you. That must be why he decided to marry you and break poor Annabella's heart like that. I must say, I was surprised, but it's obvious now. You see, you and Tessa have a lot in common.'

'I'm glad,' said Becky shortly.

'How very generous,' marvelled Judith softly, 'how very, very generous. Don't you mind having Tessa thrust upon you?'

'Of course not. I'll be happy to help her if I can.'

'Oh, I'm sure you can.' Judith smiled. 'If anyone can make her see the Shepherds in their true light, you can.'

'Me? But I don't know the Shepherds.'

'Well, not Caradoc perhaps, but Megan. And you knew Megan's husband, didn't you? After all, he's the one who really runs the place and gives those terrible parties that Tessa will insist on going to.' Her eyes narrowed, watching Becky's suddenly stricken expression with pleasure. 'She never listens to me, of course, but I'm sure you'll have more success. After all, you must be the world expert on Tony Boyd, mustn't you?'

With a final, light laugh she shouldered her way past Becky, standing as still as stone in the middle of the floor.

'Don't bother about me,' she said lightly, 'I'll go to an

hotel. You'll have your hands quite full enough with Tessa, and I wouldn't want to get in your way.' She wafted out of the house.

It quite spoiled Becky's satisfaction in having fulfilled the first of her obligations to Charles and dislodged Judith from his home.

Nevertheless, when he returned a week later she told him of her success. Charles had been looking tired, but his face broke into laughter at her air of innocent pride.

'Excellent,' he said. 'Do you think you've got rid of her for good?'

'As long as there's a chance of Tessa coming to stay at the same time,' Becky said composedly. 'It's odd. I don't get the impression that she dislikes Tessa or anything like that.'

'Oh, she doesn't; in her way she's quite fond of her. She just doesn't want to live with her.'

'Poor Tess,' said Becky compassionately.

'It's mutual, as far as I can judge.'

'Have you heard from Tessa?'

'No, she's maintaining a stony silence. She's offended with me.'

'Why?'

Charles shrugged. 'Lord knows! I only told her that she couldn't go and stay with some people this summer. If she wants to stay in London she can come here for as long as she likes and bring whoever she likes, or she could go abroad. I wouldn't mind that.'

'As long as she stays away from Caradoc Shepherd?' asked Becky, remembering Judith's malice.

He gave her a quick look. 'So you know about that.'

'I do now,' she said with resentment, 'you might have told me.'

'Yes,' he agreed, 'I should have done.'

'Was it the Shepherds she wanted to stay with this summer?'

'Yes,' he said again. 'She's at school with the younger sister: I don't know the girl's name. Tess went to stay with them at Easter because Judith wanted her home as little as possible. That was when the worst of this phase started. I think myself she'll get over it, but it worries Edward and in his present state that's not good for him. So I put my foot down. Otherwise I'd let her go and wait till she got tired of it.'

'Are you so sure she would?'

Charles raised his eyebrows. 'Naturally. Tessa's a bright creature, the Shepherds are not. She couldn't put up with their sort of inanity for two minutes if it weren't a sort of forbidden fruit. I'd give Caradoc about a week to bore her.'

'Why don't you tell your father that?'

'I did, but he didn't really believe me. He's too far away and he's got too little to do except worry about his little girl. I told him to leave Tessa in our hands and he's accepted that, but it wouldn't do for Judith to write and tell him that I was letting Tessa visit the Shepherds, however convinced I may be of Tessa's basic good sense.'

'I see.' Becky was chastened by the faint emphasis that she thought she detected on this last reference to his sister's name.

'Oh, by the way, I've got a letter for you from Edward. He was worried about not giving you an engagement present.'

Becky accepted it in surprise. Charles watched her in some amusement as she ignored the brown paper parcel and tore open the letter he presented her with, then he laughed and stretched. 'I'll leave you with your correspondence. I've got to go to Edinburgh this afternoon.'

She looked up. 'Have you? but you've only just got back.'

Charles grimaced. 'I know. I stayed longer with Edward than I intended. He was—rather down.'

'Oh dear.' Becky looked at him searchingly. 'Would it be any use if I were to write to him?'

He was looking preoccupied, but a smile broke through at that. 'I'm sure he'd love it. You're a kind child, aren't you, my love?' He buffed the back of his hand absentmindedly down her cheek. 'Look at your present. I'm going to put my papers together.'

When he had gone she opened his father's present carefully. It proved to be a long Edwardian string of pearls, in a velvet box battered and stained with age.

'I hope you like them,' Edward had written with unwonted diffidence. 'They belonged to Charles' mother, who inherited them from her grandmother. I always used to think when you were quite a small girl that they would suit you; it never occurred to me then that you and Charles might marry, though I can't deny that I often hoped for it.' He rambled on in reminiscent vein over several pages of airmail notepaper. Increasingly touched, Becky read it through slowly. At the last paragraph her eyes began to mist.

'I know you have been very unhappy, my dear,' wrote Edward, 'because your mother has told me about it— I hope you don't mind that. I was so very sorry: I do trust that now you will put all the bitterness behind you and allow Charles to make you happy.'

The paper fell out of her hands and she bent her head, knuckling her eyes like the child Charles had called her. The pearls slid to the ground unheeded, and she abandoned herself to a bout of weeping that had been threatening for months. It went on for ten exhausting minutes, at the end of which she ran out of breath and tears alike.

She could hear Charles in his study and went quickly into the kitchen to bathe her eyes. They were red and puffy and altogether too eloquent of the manner in which she had spent the interim, for her to face him just yet. Becky blew her nose on a convenient piece of kitchen roll and hoped that Charles would find enough to occupy him until the signs of weeping had subsided somewhat.

But of course he didn't.

'Becky,' he said, wandering into her sanctum, 'have you seen ... Hello,' perceiving her expression, 'what's the matter?'

'Nothing,' she said, turning away.

'You're not feeling groggy again?' he demanded, his anxiety over her accident still unallayed.

'No, of course not. I'm perfectly recovered. I—just had the sniffles.'

'Oh,' he said in quite another voice. 'Regrets setting in again?'

She stared at him. 'I don't know what you mean. If you must know, your father'—her voice became suspended—'your father sent me a string of pearls.'

'And that made you cry?'

'Well, it was so kind of him.' She sniffed and blew her nose on the tissue again. 'And he wrote me such a generous letter. I was thinking—he was the only one who's seemed really pleased.'

Charles took the tissue away from her and threw it in the trash bucket, silently replacing it with his own snowy handkerchief.

'My father's very fond of you,' he said expressionlessly. 'From his point of view, our marriage is definitely a good thing. You must make allowances for him.'

Incapable of speech, Becky nodded silently as her tears began to flow freely again. He patted her shoulder casually and left her.

When he had quitted the house for the overnight express to Edinburgh, she sat down to try to compose a letter of thanks to Edward, but she found it singularly difficult to produce anything but platitudes which Edward would immediately see through. She wondered what Charles had told him about their marriage, and decided that he must have ignored the subject as far as possible. After all, they had hardly settled into a routine yet. And anyway they would have had other things to talk about—Judith, she supposed, and certainly Tessa.

As if on cue the telephone began to ring.

It was the headmistress of Tessa's expensive penitentiary.

'She has run away,' said Mrs Winterflood baldly, 'she and that tiresome girl Marina Shepherd. Tessa said she was feeling ill at supper and was supposed to go back to her room, but instead she must have climbed over the wall. Marina had permission to go to the cinema with her brother and simply didn't come back. They must have come back to the school and waited outside until it was dark.'

'Oh, good heavens,' gasped Becky, her initial amusement at Tessa's daring swamped in dismay, 'what on earth am I to do? Tessa's brother is on the train to Edinburgh. I can't get hold of him until tomorrow morning.'

'You have my sympathy,' snapped Mrs Winterflood. 'I imagine Tessa's well on her way to London by now with the Shepherds. Really, you'd think, considering he's supposed to be an adult, Mr Shepherd would have more sense.'

'Do you think she'll still be with them, then?'

'Oh, undoubtedly, I would say. Marina and she are very —alike,' said Mrs Winterflood, sounding as if she could have chosen another adjective had she not been talking to an anxious relative.

'Have you their address? Their London address? I suppose the least I can do is get in touch with Caradoc Shepherd.'

'Well, it's his sister's address,' submitted Mrs Winterflood, obviously hoping to unload all responsibility for Tessa on to her auditor, 'a Mrs Boyd. Do you know her?'

Becky swallowed. 'Not—not personally.'

'Well, what are you going to do, Miss Summerson? Will you see Mrs Boyd, or shall I get in touch with the police and report Tessa missing?'

'Oh no, don't do that,' said Becky, horrified. She closed her eyes. The telephone was wet in her convulsive clasp. It seemed there was no other way out. 'All right, I'll go to the Boyds. Can you give me the address?'

It was, of course, on the other side of town, and with her wrist still heavily bandaged, Becky was incapable of driving. It took her an hour to find the flat and another fifteen minutes to pluck up courage to ring the bell.

The door was opened by a little dark girl of about eighteen, who, from the faint border of suds on her hastily-straightened sleeves, must have been in the middle of washing up.

'I'd like to see Mrs Boyd, please,' said Becky clearly.

'Mrs Boyd is not at home,' she was told in a strongly accented voice. 'Mr Boyd only is here.'

Becky bit her lip. 'Very well then, please may I see Mr Boyd?'

The girl looked doubtful, but at that point a door opened in the flat and Tony himself strolled out.

Unmistakably it was Tony. In the two years since she had seen him he had allowed his hair to grow a little longer, so that it now brushed his shoulders in an elegant fall which would have been very attractive on a twenty-year-old. He was heavier than she remembered, and his floridly-flowered silk shirt did not complement his naturally rosy complexion. He wore an expensive tan and an enormous emerald signet on his left hand.

When he saw her he stopped dead.

'*Becky!*'

'I'm sorry to push my way in——' she began stiffly, but he surged forward, almost pulling her into the over-heated flat in his exuberance.

'Nonsense, nonsense, it's lovely to see you. I always knew I'd meet up with you again one day, but I'd almost given up looking. Where did you spring from?'

'The past,' she said drily.

'Come and have a drink and let me look at you.' He was quite unembarrassed, she saw with amusement; there was no echo of her own trepidatious approach to an old love. He was just overwhelmingly pleased with himself, and some of his satisfaction was allowed to spill over on to her. 'You're very elegant,' he commented. 'What are you doing now?'

'Looking for my future sister-in-law,' she said literally.

'Oh, so you're going to be married?'

'Did you think I'd stay single?'

'Yes,' he said.

She chuckled, finding his conceit blessedly funny. This wasn't the devastating ogre she recalled—he was really rather a silly man.

'I'm sorry to disappoint you, then,' she retorted.

'Who are you marrying?'

'Charles Mallory,' said Becky briefly, 'and I'm here because I want to collect his sister.'

'Mallory, eh?' he whistled. 'Playing in the big league now!'

'Where's Tessa?'

He shrugged. 'Who knows? Don't ask me, I've no taste for children. If she's anywhere, she'll be with Caradoc. He's more than a little smitten.'

Becky was disgusted. 'She's only seventeen.'

Tony shrugged again, unpleasantly. 'She's a big girl, and she can look after herself. Not all women keep that schoolgirl innocence as long as you, you know.'

Her feelings must have shown themselves in her expression, because he began to look ugly.

'Look, stick around if you don't believe me. If Caradoc brings her here you're welcome to take her away if she'll go with you.'

'And if she won't?'

'What do you expect me to do about it?' he began to bluster. 'Caradoc may not bring her here anyway . . .'

He was interrupted by another ring at the doorbell.

'Sounds as if I was wrong,' he said ruefully, 'I'm not expecting anyone else. Oh God, now I suppose we're going to have an almighty row.'

Becky squared her shoulders and he looked at her, half laughing, half in reproach.

'You know, most of the time I live a peaceable existence,' he mused. 'Comfortable. Quiet, even. But whenever you crop up I find myself pitchforked into the middle of extremely uncomfortable and noisy quarrels.'

'Don't worry, Tony,' she said softly, 'I shan't crop up again. I'll just take Tessa and fade quietly from the scene.'

'That,' he said under his breath, ignoring the commotion of arrival in the hall, 'would be a pity. However unsettling you may be you were always'—he reached for her with bland self-assurance—'a sweet thing.'

For the first time in her life Becky deliberately raised her hand in anger against a fellow creature. She swung at him, an inexpert, open-handed blow with the full force of her arm behind it. It filled her with a primitive satisfaction. Tony clapped a hand to his reddening cheek, a look of almost comical incredulity in his eyes.

In the doorway, Caradoc and his sister stood, open-mouthed. Behind them Tessa Mallory looked shocked.

Becky glared at her, 'Tessa! I'm glad to see you. You are an unending nuisance, and I'm not wasting any more of my time on your tedious acquaintance. If you want to stay here, you do so on your own.'

Head high, she marched out, pushing Marina Shepherd rudely out of the way and not even looking to see if Tessa was following her.

CHAPTER NINE

Outside the block of flats Tessa said in a small voice, 'Where did you leave the car?'

'I didn't bring it. I didn't fancy trying to drive with my wrist set rigid.'

'Oh, *poor* Becky!' Suddenly and inexcusably Tessa began to giggle. Becky glared at her.

'Now what?'

'I was just thinking about Tony,' confessed Tessa. 'That was the hand you hit him with. No wonder he looked so stunned. There must be a few pounds of plaster of Paris in that cast.'

'Good God!' Becky too began to laugh. 'I hope I haven't done him any irreparable damage.'

'Oh, you've probably addled his brains permanently,' said Tessa cheerfully. 'No one will notice.'

Becky stared. 'I thought he was a friend of yours.'

'I,' said Tessa, suddenly sounding very like her brother, 'might have said the same of you.'

'Ouch,' said Becky goodhumouredly. 'Not any longer.'

'That goes for me too,' Tessa announced.

'And Caradoc?'

They had come to the Underground and Becky plunged down it. Tessa paused.

'I haven't any money.'

'I'll pay your fare,' Becky assured her. 'Did you run away without money?'

'No. I took some money and some clothes too, of course, but they're all in Caradoc's car. You didn't,' Tessa pointed out, 'give me very much time to retrieve them.'

'No, I suppose I didn't,' said Becky, conscience-stricken. 'Poor old Tess! I was so angry I didn't stop to think.'

'Yes, I could see that, and anyway it doesn't matter. We can send Charles round to collect my belongings,' said Tessa, blithely disposing of the absent Mr Mallory's precious time. 'Perhaps he'll beat up Tony Boyd,' she added hopefully.

Becky choked with laughter. 'You're very bloodthirsty. Why do you want violence to ensue?'

Tessa shifted her shoulders. 'Oh, they're so *unreal*. They pose and titter and cheat. They're boring, and they spend all their time talking about money.'

Becky forbore to remind her that she had wanted to spend the summer with the Shepherds, judging that she had had an illuminating ride to London in Marina and Caradoc's company. However, she couldn't resist inquiring, 'But why should Charles beat up Tony?'

'Oh, because he attacked you,' Tessa said in thrilling accents. She contemplated her vision of the scene with evident satisfaction. 'And so I shall tell him.'

'Tony?' said Becky, quite bewildered.

'Charles.'

'You are not,' said Becky with the resolution of panic, 'to tell Charles anything at all.'

'Why not?'

'Because he doesn't know you've run away from school, for a start. He's in Edinburgh for the night. He will—would—be absolutely furious. You can go back tomorrow and I'll buy that Winterflood woman's silence. After all, there's only another ten days or so to go and then you can come home anyway.'

'No,' said Tessa mutinously.

Becky fed coins into a ticket machine and urged Tessa through the barrier.

'Please don't be difficult, Tess. I promise you you shan't

go back next term if you don't want to, but don't go and pull everything round your ears for the sake of ten days.'

'You sound like Charles,' said Tessa, losing her friendliness.

A train came rushing out of its tunnel and they ran for it. They flung themselves aboard just as the doors were closing and Becky ran an agitated hand through her hair, peering at the unfamiliar underground map on the train roof.

'Where do we have to change?' she said, half to herself.

Tessa gave the map a cursory glance. 'Charing Cross,' she said, dismissing it. 'Listen, Becky, I'm not going back to that place and you can't make me.'

'No, of course I can't. I wouldn't try.'

'Then why talk about it in the first place?'

'Tessa, you've already run away from one school. I understand, believe me, I'm not exactly a stranger to running away myself, though I wouldn't have had the courage to do it at your age. But even though I don't blame you, I can't help knowing that it doesn't look very good.'

'Look!' Tessa was contemptuous. 'To whom?'

'To an interviewer, for a start.' Becky looked at the sulky little face from which the make-up was already beginning to flake away. 'Do you want to go to university? Or a sixth-form college?' with some memory of Mrs Summerson's gossip. 'So do too many other people. If they think you might not be able to stick the course they won't waste a place on you.'

Tessa pinched her lips together, obviously suspicious of the argument.

'Of course, your father has plenty of money, and he could send you to some finishing school if he wanted.

Lots of cookery lessons and things,' said Becky with lofty disdain. She found that Tessa's mutinous expression had given way to a thoughtful frown.

'That's what Mother wants.'

'What?'

'Me to go to a finishing school. It would kill two birds with one stone, you see, get me out of the country and introduce me to nice people. Well, what she thinks are nice people.'

'Oh,' said Becky noncommittally.

'Mother,' said Tessa with a sideways glance under her lashes at her companion, 'quite liked the Shepherds.'

'Oh yes?'

'Daddy didn't, though.'

'I'm not surprised,' avowed Becky.

'Nor am I now.' Tessa gave a little wriggle in her seat like a puppy, and with one of her abrupt changes of mood became confiding again. 'Tony had a cheek thinking he could paw you about just because you used to be engaged to him.' She bit her thumbnail, 'I do wish,' she added wistfully, 'that I'd thought of slapping Caradoc's face.'

'Why? Did he give you cause?' asked Becky, startled.

'Well, no,' agreed Tessa reluctantly, 'but it would have been such a marvellous thing to do.' She regarded her future sister-in-law with admiration.

'I'm glad you think so. I'm thoroughly ashamed of myself,' Becky replied crushingly. She spoilt her effect by adding, 'He did look silly, didn't he?'

They laughed heartlessly and finished the journey very good friends.

The house, when they reached it, was lit up.

'Hullo,' said Tessa. 'Did you forget to turn all the lights off?'

Becky shook her head. 'No. Anyway, I never had that many on.'

'Perhaps Charles has come back?'

'I don't see how he could, he was going to catch the sleeper. Perhaps it's your mother. That woman must have telephoned her too.'

'Do you think so?' Tessa was surprised that Becky might consider such a manifestation of maternal concern at all likely. 'I don't really,' she confessed, 'feel like a row with Mother tonight.'

'Then we'll go in the back door and sneak up the stairs,' said Becky, recklessly committing her support.

Tessa's eyes gleamed. 'Can we?'

'Of course. If I've got the back door key with me, of course.'

Tessa found this very poor-spirited and was perfectly prepared to climb in the scullery window, but fortunately this proved to be unnecessary. They tiptoed up the stairs, past the drawing room and Charles' newly converted study to the room Becky was preparing for Tessa.

'It's not tidy because we didn't expect you quite yet,' Becky apologised, 'and it's not decorated because I thought you might prefer to have a say in that yourself. But at least the bed's made up.'

Enchanted to be apologised to and happy to camp in the middle of cardboard boxes and spare furniture, Tessa received a spare nightdress of Becky's with every appearance of delight. 'I'm glad you're marrying Charles,' she decided, rubbing her face against the silk.

'Run through your mother's wardrobe?' Becky inquired drily, not unduly elated by the compliment.

'It will be nice to have another stock to borrow from,' Tessa replied sedately.

'At the moment I should think the first thing you want to borrow is cleanser,' observed Becky.

Tessa wrinkled her nose in the mirror. 'I've had a hard day,' she excused her peeling maquillage.

'You have indeed. Are you hungry?'

'No, Caradoc bought us dinner and I had heaps. It was marvellous. School had stew for supper. Stew!' said Tessa, bouncing experimentally on the bed. 'Ugh! If you don't eat it in twenty seconds it congeals under your eyes.' She cast a tragically reproachful glance on Becky. 'And you want me to go *back* there.'

'I'll pack you a hamper to take with you,' Becky soothed her.

'That's blackmail,' Tessa informed her, 'or undue influence or something. Charles would know.'

Becky stared at her with undisguised horror. 'Don't tell me you're another lawyer.'

'Would you throw me out if I were?' asked Tessa with interest.

'I doubt if Charles would let me,' Becky said gloomily.

Tessa threw a pillow at her. 'You're so welcoming,' she mocked, 'it really makes me feel wanted.'

Her hostess caught the pillow and chuckled. Tessa flung herself back on the bed, looking at Becky under her lashes. This was the first occasion that she had really had much to do with her; before the holiday she had looked depressed and irritable and since returning from the island Tessa had other things to occupy her mind. Now she discovered the fugitive charm in her future sister-in-law, and she ceased to wonder why Charles wanted to marry her. At the same time the dark suspicion that her mother might be right, and Becky be imported into the Mallory family as a reforming agent for herself, evaporated.

'I'll tell you what,' she offered, 'I'll agree not to be a lawyer if you'll agree not to make me do good works.'

Becky stared.

'Mother,' said Tessa, primming her mouth, 'said you were going to Reform me.'

'I'll spare you the soup kitchens,' said Becky drily.

'In that case,' Tessa responded graciously, 'I accept your pressing invitation.'

'God help me!' Becky tossed the pillow back. 'You know where the bathroom is. If you change your mind about food, I'll be in the kitchen.'

She went downstairs, switching the lights off as she went. It was very odd that they should all come to be on like this. She could only assume some electrical disaster, as there was no sign of Judith Mallory. Fortunately nothing fused as she flicked the switches.

On impulse she decided to listen to some music before she went to bed; soothing music and a final cigarette might, she thought wryly, do something to calm her whirling brain. Head down, she pushed open the door of the drawing room, which stood slightly ajar as if someone had quitted the room too preoccupied to notice.

But they had not left the room. They were still there, locked fast in each other's arms.

Becky stopped dead, her eyes flaring with shock.

Charles, half turned away from the door, was holding Annabella Smart in a comprehensive embrace. The lady stood on tiptoe, and her excellently manicured fingers, Becky observed with detached interest, were flexing themselves in his hair like the claws of a contented cat.

It was a scene too intimate to be witnessed. After one paralysed moment, Becky stepped back, but not quite quickly enough.

In the midst of their mutual absorption they had somehow detected her presence. Annabella froze. Charles, one hand going almost absentmindedly to detach her clinging arms, lifted his head and turned to the doorway; his hair was tousled and he was breathing hard. Em-

165

barrassed, and more than that, Becky went instantly into full retreat.

'I'm frightfully sorry,' she muttered, backing. 'I shouldn't have—I mean, I didn't know anyone was here. I thought you'd gone, Charles.'

He stared at her blankly. She found she was shaking and put an unsteady hand out to the nearest object for support. It chanced to be the doorknob, and she leant on it heavily.

She made herself draw a steadying breath and tried again. 'I—I was looking for a cigarette.' Under her weight the door moved outwards a little and she staggered. So slight a thing could discompose her, she found. She gasped, a harsh, quickly suppressed reaction, out of all proportion to the incident. Her heart was pounding almost painfully against her rib cage and she put her hand to her side to ease it. Closing her eyes briefly, she fought for self-control. 'I'm sorry,' she said again. 'Forgive me.'

She retreated in fairly good order from the drawing room, pulling the door gently to behind her. Then, dignity falling from her with some rapidity, she fled up the stairs, one flight to the comparative safety of the darkened first floor, two flights to her bedroom and home.

It never occurred to her that Charles would follow her. There was Annabella, after all, to be soothed, mollified and, presumably, reassured. Without giving any precise thought to the scene she had left behind her in the drawing-room, Becky assumed vaguely that Charles would assure Annabella that, despite the temporary embarrassment, no lasting harm had been done. His fiancée was in no position to complain about his conduct, and in any event she was quite indifferent to it. All Becky was aware of, dismayingly, was that she was very far from indifferent.

She gave an involuntary cry, part childish fury, part wholly adult pain. Of course, she wasn't in the least indifferent and hadn't been for weeks! She found she could have sobbed aloud.

Unguardedly she sank on to her dressing stool, her hand to her mouth. The feelings of shame, impatience and grief that assailed her were like a physical onslaught, and Becky leant forward with her head in her hands.

She did not hear the door open, and so Charles discovered her.

'*Becky!*' For a moment he sounded panic-stricken and quite unlike his normal unruffled self.

She did not turn. She found, slightly to her surprise, that she was crying, and didn't want him to see her tears. When he switched on the lamp on the dressing-table beside her she flinched away from it. He stood watching her almost helplessly.

'Becky,' he said again, more quietly, 'are you all right?'

She dropped her hands and looked at them, folded tightly in her lap. 'Yes, thank you,' she said in a wooden little voice.

'Are you sure?' He hesitated a moment and then dropped a hand on her hunched shoulder. 'You look——'

She flashed a quick defiant look up at him. His mouth twitched. 'Well?' she demanded.

'Rather fraught,' he supplied. With one finger he touched her cheek gently. The traces of tears were very clear.

'So would you,' said Becky, her voice not quite breaking, 'if you'd had the day I have.'

The tears welled up again, most inconsiderately, and she sniffed. Charles silently handed her a large white handkerchief.

'Thank you.' She mopped her eyes, dried her cheeks and blew her nose hard.

Looking up, she found him regarding her with a very strange expression. Confused, she blew her nose again, and his eyes began to dance. He went down on his haunches in front of her and took the handkerchief from her limp grasp.

'Sometimes,' he said very softly, 'I have the greatest difficulty in remembering that you're no longer a child.'

She was hurt. 'Don't laugh at me,' she said sharply.

'Laugh at you?' he echoed. He applied the handkerchief to a pathetic smudge of blotted mascara on her left cheekbone. 'I wouldn't dare.'

'Yes, you would,' said Becky resentfully. 'You've always laughed at me.'

'Then you can't expect me to stop now,' he said outrageously, and smiled at her very kindly. 'Better now?'

'No!' she snapped.

'What? Not got your breath back yet? Shall I get you a brandy?'

Becky shuddered. 'No, you know I hate the stuff. Anyway, brandy doesn't do anything for tiredness. There's nothing wrong with me that twenty-four hours' sleep won't cure.'

His eyes narrowed. 'Isn't there?'

She glared at him. 'What should be?'

'Well, forgive me if I've made a mistake, but I thought you'd had something of a shock.'

Becky set her teeth. 'You mean interrupting you and Annabella like that?'

He didn't answer that directly. 'You went white,' he said reflectively, 'I've read about it, but never actually seen it happen before. You looked like a ghost.'

'How very disconcerting for you,' she commiserated.

'Rather more than that,' he said ruefully, 'I was worried.'

He would have continued, but she interrupted. 'Then I

owe you an apology. There's no need to worry—it was unfortunate, but it was quite as much my fault as yours. I had no business to be barging in like that.'

'Hadn't you?'

'No, and I'm very sorry. I wouldn't have embarrassed you for the world.'

This very handsome apology did not seem to placate him as it should have done. For an instant, thought Becky, quailing, he looked as angry as she had ever seen him; then he drew away from her and stood up.

'As you say, the blame is about equally divided. I thought you would be in bed. You're not usually up as late as this.'

'No,' she agreed miserably.

His eyes grew keen. 'So why are you tonight? I assume you weren't lying in wait for me?'

Becky flushed and in her turn stood up. 'I wouldn't *spy* on you,' she said proudly.

Charles sighed. 'I didn't suggest that you would, I simply thought you might have something you wanted to discuss and have waited up for me to do so.' He put his hands on her shoulders and pulled her towards him. 'Becky, why is it that I can't say the most innocent thing to you, without you misinterpreting it?'

'I don't think——' she began stiffly, but he didn't let her finish.

'Oh, but you do, that's the trouble. If you thought a bit less and listened a bit more we might deal together much more comfortably.'

'Don't be so smug,' snapped Becky. 'I listened to you this afternoon when you told me you were going to Edinburgh, and look what happens. Even you can't pretend that it was my fault.'

'I wouldn't want to.' He took her agitated hands and held them in a firm clasp against his chest. 'Becky, my dear fool, will you *listen* to me? I was worried when I left you, you were so lachrymose. I couldn't get it out of my head. So when I got to the station I telephoned Annabella and asked her to come over and see whether you were all right.'

'That,' said Becky with heavy irony, 'was thoughtful of you.'

'She found the place empty as if you'd rushed out— or been dragged, she thought, and she was alarmed. She knew I expected you to be there. She got through to me at the station and I came home.' He lifted her chin. 'I was going to come anyway,' he said softly. 'I couldn't have slept all the way to Scotland thinking about you crying like that.'

'You're too kind,' she said, unmollified.

'You have every right to be angry,' he allowed, making a great effort to keep his temper.

'I'm glad you see that at any rate!'

'You're not making things easier . . .'

'Why should I make things easier for you? You haven't exactly overwhelmed *me* with consideration,' she snapped.

'Don't be childish.'

'It isn't childish,' said Becky with great restraint, 'to wish that you would conduct your private affairs somewhere other than under my nose.'

'Yes, it is, very childish. Annabella Smart is hardly my private affair.'

'Then she should be. It's most unpleasant to find these things in public.'

'Becky, stop it. I agree I haven't behaved well tonight, but I was worried about you and . . .'

'Are you trying to say you were wrapped in Annabella's arms because you were worried about me?' she demanded incredulous at his effrontery.

'God, you're hidebound! Can't you unlock your mind, just the tiniest bit?'

'Believe your story, you mean?'

'Would that be so terrible?'

'Yes,' said Becky flatly. Shock had given place to blazing anger. 'I've made my own decisions and formed my own views all my life, and I'm not going to spend the rest of it looking at the world through a pair of glasses that you've made for me.'

He looked amused. 'That wasn't quite what I was suggesting.'

'Wasn't it?' She glared at him. 'Look, Charles, there are some women—I've met them—who will say black is white if some man tells them so.'

'You think that's what I want you to do?' he said curiously.

'Well, don't you?'

He shook his head sorrowfully. 'You always misjudge me.'

She was shaking with anger while he was still quite composed. She found she hated him with a force that she had believed lost with childhood. 'I certainly don't share your own high opinion of yourself,' she said nastily. 'You're hardly omniscient, Charles.'

His eyebrows flew up. 'I've never claimed to be.'

'No? So on what grounds do you want to dictate to me what I should think?'

'I *don't* want to dictate to you.' He was beginning to sound grim, 'I'd just like a hearing sometimes. I have a right to be heard.'

'You think so?' she said, dangerously quiet.

'Becky——'

'After what I've been told, after what I've just seen myself downstairs, you think you have the right to lecture me?' He uttered an explosive exclamation but she was too angry to stop. 'Let me make myself clear. We had an agreement which I thought you understood; it included no right on your part to interfere in my life in any way. Do you hear? No right at all.'

He smiled, not pleasantly. 'You're mistaken,' he said with composure.

His hands closed like a vice on her arms. Preoccupied as she was with her own fury, Becky had not observed that Charles too had lost his temper; his eyes were black with it and his mouth was a thin vicious line. Now her head reared back and she stared at him in disbelief. She tried to pull away.

'No,' she said faintly, protesting as much at the unforgiving anger she saw in his face as at the pain in her arms.

He ignored her; alarmed, she wondered whether he had even heard her. He shook her a couple of times and then, as if suddenly overcome by impatience, wrenched her into his arms.

He kissed her with an abandon for which she was wholly unprepared. Nothing had ever led her to suspect that Charles, always so coolly master of himself and the situation, would ever permit himself to be stampeded out of his habitual calm. Even on that memorable evening when some demon of mischief had prompted him to make love to her, she had been aware of a strong vein of mockery running through his conversation. Whether he had mocked her, or himself, or even the heavily romantic atmosphere, she had been too confused to determine. But she had judged that whatever his private feelings might be, they had remained firmly under control.

But now that control had been flung aside and with it, she found, the last vestige of her immunity to him.

At first she fought strenuously against his hold. It was

pure instinct—she had been kissed often enough before not to fly into a panic.

In ordinary circumstances she would have responded politely and then, with gentle and quite unanswerable decision, dismissed him. It was a technique that had accounted quite satisfactorily for John Townsend and any other intrusive young man brave enough to venture in spite of the warning signs. It had not repelled Charles on an earlier occasion, but she had been tired and thrown off balance by weeks of tension. Today she had no such excuse. And never before had she forgot her dignity so far as to enter into a tussle like some frightened school-girl kissed for the first time.

But she found she was frightened, though she could not say of what, and she might just as well have been Tessa's age, for all the poise left her. Her head began to swim and soon she was clinging to him as the only steady thing in a wildly rocking universe. His arms tightened and she gave herself up to the unexpectedly sweet exhilaration.

Finally, when she was quiet and clinging, he raised his head and considered her thoughtfully.

'We should,' he said, his voice husky but otherwise unmistakably his old sardonic tone, 'have done that a long time ago.'

She swallowed shakily.

He chuckled. 'Truce?'

She closed her eyes and drew away from him. 'No,' she said in an uneven voice. Her throat felt dry. 'No. No, no, no!'

'I am not,' Charles told her with great patience, 'going to squabble with you any more this evening. I'm much too tired. Either you simmer down or I leave you.'

'Do that,' she told him bitterly, 'permanently.' She walked away from him, astonished to find that her knees were shaking. 'Go on. Annabella must be waiting for you.'

He started forward. 'Annabella means nothing to me.'

'That,' she said very nastily, 'is your problem. Go away.'

'Oh, Becky,' he said sorrowfully, 'you just don't give me a chance.'

'Go away,' she repeated, pressing her hands together to stop their trembling. 'I *hate* you!'

She said it with conviction. Looking round at him, she discovered that he believed her. He gave a little half-shrug of resignation and smiled lopsidedly.

'I can see you do. Very clearly.' His voice was full of self-mockery. 'If that's what you want—I'll go.' He paused at the door as if hoping she would say something, but her voice was wholly suspended and her eyes full of anger. Charles said softly, 'Goodbye, Becky.'

CHAPTER TEN

BECKY'S first instinct was to take the coward's way: to pack her bags and retreat again into oblivion. For a longing few moments she contemplated flight. John Townsend would receive her kindly; Charles, even if he made the attempt, would be unlikely to discover her if John agreed to hide her. It tempted her inordinately.

But then common sense reasserted itself. There was Tessa to consider—she had only just arrived. No hostess worthy the name would leave a guest to fend for herself simply because she had some small family disagreement.

But it wasn't a small disagreement, objected Becky's secret self miserably, it was a quarrel of devastating proportions. She, who had been baiting Charles Mallory all her life, had never imagined it would be possible to provoke him so disastrously.

Musing on the extent of that disaster, Becky at last faced the truth that she had been skirting, she thought, all her life. Charles was necessary to her. She could not contemplate life without him. His wit, his style had formed a cornerstone in the view of life she had built for herself. For years she had been measuring other men against his image, and always she had found them wanting. Her very passion for Tony had been a perverse distortion of this perspective. Because Tony had been so helplessly inadequate, so utterly inferior to the capable Mallory, she had thrown herself headlong into his defence. Charles could meet the world on its own terms and win; Tony Boyd needed special pleading.

Becky, recognising her own motives and not liking the taste of them, began to pace the floor.

She spent a desperate night, not even bothering to go to bed, so certain was she that sleep would elude her. She tried to resolve her problems, but all that her stubborn brain would do was reiterate that Charles must somehow be induced to modify his sentence. He *could* not send her away. And yet—and yet—his farewell had sounded chillingly final. It rang in her ears. And she had deserved it, asked for it, positively demanded it, in her ungovernable rage.

She was heavy-eyed and preoccupied when she greeted Tessa across the breakfast table the following morning.

'How am I going to get back to that place?' demanded Tessa, after a particularly long silence during which Becky had sat crumbling bread between her fingers and staring drearily into space.

'I'll drive you,' said Becky, who had not thought about it.

'But what about your wrist?'

'It'll be all right, I expect. If I have a disaster you'll have to step into the breach.'

Tessa, who had just begun to learn to drive, was perfectly willing.

'But what about getting back?' she asked dubiously.

'Perhaps I won't come back.'

'*What?*'

'Oh, forget it,' said Becky. 'Hurry up, I want to get started.'

Of Charles there was no sign; presumably he had resumed his interrupted journey to Edinburgh. There was no letter, as she had half hoped, half feared, waiting for her on the hall table. Whatever he had in mind, he was obviously not going to enlighten her.

Becky reversed the car out of the garage with difficulty. Her stiffly bandaged arm impeded her more than she had hoped, and she was glad enough to surrender the steering wheel to Tessa once they were on the open road. It answered very well. Tessa had had sufficient lessons to be a very competent driver as long as she was not presented with any mechanical crises or undue traffic, and Becky was able to let her mind wander. For Tessa it clearly made up in no small degree for being returned to school ignominiously. In fact she drove through the double iron gates with considerable dash and swished Charles' powerful car to a halt outside the main entrance with something suspiciously like complacence.

Briefly, Becky made her excuses to Mrs Winterflood, who was not going to chide too harshly the guardian of a child whose parents paid as lavishly as did the Mallorys for the dubious refinements of her establishment. Becky disliked her instantly and irremediably, and determined to do her utmost to persuade Charles that Tessa should leave her care.

Not that her words were likely to carry any weight with him, she told herself glumly. She had lost any right she might have to try to influence him by her outburst last night. Before that he might have listened to her, out of courtesy or kindness. It was truly remarkable, she reflected in elegiac mood, how very kind to her he had been, considering that he was not by nature a patient man. She must have done much to try his patience—in fact, it was a mystery why he had allowed his bluff to be called so far as to engage himself to marry such an obviously unsatisfactory wife. Filled with compunction, she began to reproach herself.

At that point she had a puncture, and the sudden intrusion of mechanics into her mood of gentle melancholy was disconcerting. Stopping the car, she got out and surveyed the damage in some dudgeon. The back offside wheel subsided under her affronted eyes and the car tilted drunkenly. In her haste to pull up, she had driven too close to the verge of the country lane she had been absently travelling, and now the car slid slowly and humiliatingly into the ditch.

Becky swore.

The lane, which had attracted her by its rural absence of other traffic, now looked desolate. She had been meandering, not taking much notice of roads other than to assure herself she was moving generally in the right direction. She now found she had absolutely no idea where she was, and spent a frustrating while peering at the ungrateful map. When this vouchsafed no inspiration she determined to walk.

She had noticed no habitation on the road on which she had come, and so elected to go forward rather than back. If she couldn't find a garage, she reasoned, she might at least track down a telephone and thence call a breakdown service.

It was a long walk. The midsummer air was very pleasant to bask in but less so, she found, on a five-mile hike. Very soon her shoes raised a blister on her heel and at last, in a fury, she kicked them off and walked barefoot in the weedy margin. By the time she reached the village to which the lane made its way, sheer discomfort had overcome her languishings.

The breakdown service could not have been more disobliging. Help was promised, grudgingly, only after she had served a probationary period of anything up to three hours. Declining to trudge back to the car and wait in the heat, Becky installed herself in the otherwise deserted snug of the only pub the village boasted.

And was found there by an anxious Charles.

She heard the commotion of his arrival, but took it to be some remote village affair and nothing to do with her. Not stirring from her comfortable perch on the window seat which looked into a charming garden, she calmly went on eating and drinking and leafing idly through one of the battered paperbacks from the snug's bookshelves.

The voices outside were intrusive; a door banged and she heard a question flung out like a challenge by the new arrival. Several voices answered and there was a flurry of activity, but she ignored it placidly until the ancient wooden door of the snug was sent crashing back on its hinges and Charles stormed into the room.

Instantly she was on her feet, excuses crowding into her brain. She had done so much that was inexcusable: screamed at him like a fishwife, hidden his sister from him, driven his car into a ditch.

'What in the name of hell's delight,' he demanded between shut teeth, 'do you think you're doing?'

The door swung gently to behind him.

Becky blushed and hung her head.

'I'm very sorry ...'

'*Sorry?*' It ripped out at her. 'You take off into the middle of next week without so much as the grace to let me know you're going, and you have the gall to say you're *sorry*?'

She quailed. 'I—I—er—thought you were in Scotland.'

'So I gather,' he said furiously. 'So I should be, damn it! And if I had been, you'd have skipped wouldn't you? Packed your bags and done a bunk like a blasted schoolgirl. For the last time, Becky, I will not have it. You have got to grow up.'

She blinked under the accusations raining about her.

'I don't know what you mean.'

'Yes, you do, and I won't put up with it any more. I stood back and let you run away last time because I thought you'd been hurt and wanted to lick your wounds in private. And look what happened! You almost married Townsend.'

'No, I didn't.'

'Don't interrupt. You are the most extraordinarily in-efficient woman I've ever met. You seem to have no sense of self-preservation. The moment anything goes wrong, you just stand still and let the world hit you, then up sticks and away!'

'I don't ...'

'Well, I've had enough. Lord knows I never wanted to dictate to you, as you seem to think, or run your life either, but don't forget it's my life too, now. And you are not,' said Charles reaching for her with determina-tion, 'running out on me again.'

'I wasn't running out,' protested Becky, quite be-wildered.

That gave him pause.

'No? Are you sure?'

She whisked herself away from him indignantly. 'Of course I'm sure. I don't deny ...'

He pounced on it. 'What? That you were planning to disappear again?'

'I've got your car,' she pointed out. 'I'd hardly steal your car to run away from you.'

'Oh, perhaps you weren't going quite yet?' he asked ironically.

She sighed. 'I was taking Tessa back to school. You didn't know because I didn't have time to tell you, but she tried to run away from that school last night. I—er—collected her, put her up for the night and I've just taken her back there.'

He looked at her through narrowed eyes. As always when he was in a temper his eyes had darkened, and now they gave off flinty sparks like jet. Inwardly Becky quailed, then she raised her chin under that merciless scrutiny.

'I know,' he said softly, surprising her, 'I've just seen Tessa.'

'Oh! But how ...?'

'She and I met at the breakfast table this morning before I went to the office to get someone to stand in for me in Edinburgh.'

Becky was bewildered. 'She didn't tell me.'

'Perhaps she didn't think you'd be interested. She told me about your rescuing her—she found it very impressive, I gather.'

Thinking of the scene on which Tessa had walked in the previous night, Becky blushed.

'She should have told me,' she muttered. 'She didn't say a word on the way down.'

'That's hardly surprising. She thought you might be contemplating suicide, and she was terrified.'

Becky stared at him. 'Oh, what rubbish,' she gasped. 'Tessa was as pleased as Punch to be driving the car. She didn't think anything of the sort!'

'Oh yes, she did. You told her this morning that you might not be coming back to London, didn't you?'

Casting her mind back, Becky had to agree that some such indiscreet exclamation had passed her lips.

'So she telephoned me from school, as soon as you dropped her. Not,' he added grimly, 'that it was any surprise to me. I've been expecting you to take off ever since you said you'd marry me.'

'Have—*have* you?' Becky sat down heavily on the old wooden settle, her mind in a turmoil. 'But if you wanted to call it off, why didn't you say so?' she asked, hurt. 'Why let it go so far ...? Oh, I don't understand you, Charles.'

There was a pause and then he said in an odd voice, 'No, you don't, do you? Not the slightest little bit.'

Becky closed her eyes and leant her head back against

the wood in despair. 'I'm sorry,' she whispered.

Charles came and sat down beside her, taking possession of her hands very deliberately and running his thumb across her knuckles in a rhythmical caress. Opening her eyes, she found his head was bent and he was surveying their clasped hands absorbedly.

'I didn't say I wanted to call it off,' he murmured, almost absently, 'I said I thought you would want to. In fact I thought you would do so the moment you found out I was in love with you.'

She was stunned. She tried to speak and discovered that her voice had wholly deserted her, so she continued to stare at his bent head in silence.

'Only you didn't find out, did you? You were so busy telling your mother what a practical solution it was to her problems as well as yours! You were so busy convincing your sister that love was an adolescent aberration—above all you were so busy declaiming to the world how sensible we were that you just didn't take the time to notice that I am not—and never have been—sensible about you.'

'Charles——' she began in a strangled voice, but he hardly seemed to hear her.

'No, you'd better let me finish now I've started. I should have done it weeks ago, if I hadn't been so frightened it would scare you away. Weeks!' He laughed bitterly. 'I ought to have done it two years ago when you left Boyd.'

'No!' she protested.

'You might as well hear me out, now I've started. Then you can run away and pretend it never happened,' he said ironically. 'The truth is, Becky, that I didn't talk you into this for any of the artificial and highly convincing reasons that you have concocted in that fertile brain of yours. I wanted to marry you because I loved you. I've loved you for a long time, but I've never got close enough before. When you threw down that challenge'—he sighed—'well, at the time it seemed a heaven-sent opportunity. I shouldn't have done it, I suppose; it wasn't very chivalrous when I knew you didn't love me. But we had spent so long like a couple of planets circling at different speeds—whenever we coincided there was something pulling us apart. I thought this time I'd better take my chance when it was offered me.'

'I didn't know,' said Becky in a small ashamed voice.

His grin was wry. 'I know you didn't. I couldn't believe it. Any other woman would have realised years ago, but not you. You went right on worshipping the memory of Tony Boyd and looking neither to right nor left.'

'I—oh, I'd been hurt,' said Becky defensively. 'Don't you understand that?'

'Do you think I hadn't?' he said gently. 'Of course I understand.'

'I've been very selfish,' she said remorsefully.

'Not unduly. A little blind, perhaps.'

'More than that. I'm sorry, Charles.' She was twisting her hands together miserably. 'It's no excuse to say I didn't know, because I should have known, and I should certainly never have said I'd marry you, however briefly. It was a shocking thing to do.'

His mouth twitched. 'Certainly your mother thought so.'

'My mother?' she asked, bewildered.

'I went to see her,' he explained. 'I thought she had a right to know about her own affairs, so I went down to Almcote to tell her my father's decision about that loan he made her. She hardly listened, then she gave me a formidable lecture on making a public spectacle of you.'

Becky's brow lightened somewhat. 'She gave me a similar lecture on making a public spectacle of myself. I rather gathered that she thought you'd behaved quite well in comparison.'

'She didn't tell me that. I suppose it would have

weakened her case. Anyway, she drove me into a corner and I ended up admitting that my intentions were strictly honourable, and that if I could I would do my best to persuade you to forget all the foolishness and marry me in all seriousness.'

'Poor Mama! She must have collapsed in despair.'

A lurking smile in his eyes confused Becky, and she looked away.

'On the contrary, she laughed like a drain and said we deserved each other.'

'But she doesn't like you,' exclaimed Becky unthinkingly.

'No,' he agreed, with unimpaired calm, 'not normally. She is not, however, the sort of mother to despise any man who has the good taste to be besotted about one of her daughters. Therein lay my greatest appeal—though unfortunately not for the daughter in question. But I was determined not to give up, so that in my turn I drove you into a corner, didn't I, my poor child?'

'Me? How?'

'I forced you to retaliate. But when you actually *told* me you wouldn't put up with second best, I realised how hopeless it was.'

Becky swallowed. 'Oh.'

'Though I suppose I should have known that already. I mean, it was obvious that Townsend was up to his ears in love with you, and you were fond of him, protective, even. If you'd wanted second best, you'd have done a great deal better with him than with me, and you decided against it. I should have taken the hint.'

'I see. I've been very stupid. I hadn't realised you—er—knew about John.'

His smile was twisted. 'Becky, my dear, I've been watching you and John Townsend like a hawk for months, as far as I was able. I had spies staked out all over France. I used to phone old friends for no other reason except to find out whether you'd been seen with him; in fact, it's amazing that nobody but your mother found me out.'

Becky said with difficulty, 'I was very lonely when I first went to France, and John was kind. More than kind, he used to look after me. It was—very reassuring after what had happened at home. But it was no more than that.'

'No?'

'No,' she said firmly. 'Oh, he chose to think he was in love with me, but he wasn't really. He relied on me for moral support, that's all.'

'It's a great deal to a man like John Townsend,' he said.

'Yes, perhaps, but not enough to build anything permanent on. Not, at any rate,' said Becky, looking him between the eyes, 'to me.'

'I wish I'd known that,' Charles said thoughtfully. 'I didn't think you had a specific objection to Townsend, just to every man who wasn't Tony Boyd; and when it came to me, all those childhood resentments on top of that. You wouldn't listen to me or even see me as I was, and I couldn't get through to you at all. And then you fell down that damned cliff and I knew it was all my fault.'

Becky sat up very straight. 'Rubbish,' she said firmly.

He laughed gently. 'Don't be kind to me, Becky. I know I was pretty unforgivable. If I hadn't made you so angry ...'

'It had nothing to do with me being angry,' Becky told him. 'I thought I heard you fall and I was horrified, so I went pelting down that path without looking where I was going, and it was quite my own fault.'

His fingers tightened on hers. 'You might have been killed.'

'Unlikely,' she said astringently. 'And if I had been it wouldn't have been your fault—I was the one that was stupid. When I said I couldn't endure second best, it wasn't Tony I was thinking of at all. It was your Miss Smart.'

'Annabella?' In the blankest amazement, Charles stared at her. 'But why?'

'Charles,' said Becky patiently, 'as you say, we've known one another a long time, and during that time I have seen you with a pretty fair collection of ladies, most of them very much in the Annabella Smart mould. You seemed to have a strong degree of—shall we say understanding?—with her. You'd taken her to your island, she'd bought my clothes. I didn't believe—didn't even contemplate—that you might have fallen in love with me. On the other hand, I had every reason to suppose that you hadn't changed your habits.'

'Which included friendships with people like Annabella?'

'More than that,' demurred Becky. 'You seemed quite devoted.'

He stared at her, fascinated. 'You're even more tortuous than I thought you were. Didn't it ever occur to you, my love, that I never married anyone like Annabella Smart?'

'That didn't mean you didn't want to,' she pointed out. 'I thought you'd decided that you needed a guardian for Tessa, and elected me for the job.'

Charles dropped his head in his hands in mock despair. 'And you really *believed* that rubbish?'

'It seemed the most reasonable explanation,' Becky defended herself, 'there was no other obvious solution. I couldn't imagine that you loved me.'

He looked at her very steadily. 'Why not?'

'You never said so,' she replied simply.

'And you needed it spelt out?'

She stood up and went a little away from him, twisting her hands together in distress. 'I—I've never been able to trust my own instincts,' she confessed in a low voice. 'I only half did, with Tony, and I was proved wrong. With you—when it mattered so much more—if I'd been wrong, I couldn't have borne it. I didn't dare let myself believe that you loved me in case it was just wish-fulfilment.'

'Becky, you're a fool,' he said calmly.

'I know. Oh, I know, but I was so afraid!'

'Of me?'

'Of putting myself in your power,' she said soberly, 'if you didn't love me. And I was nearly sure you didn't. After all, why should you?'

To her indignation she discovered he was laughing. He came to her, eyes gleaming with it, and took her in his arms. 'Why indeed?'

Her head drooped hopelessly on to his shoulder. 'Well, why? When you've got Annabella.'

'I have not,' he murmured, kissing her ear thoughtfully, 'got Annabella. I was briefly and unsuccessfully tackled last night, but I got away. I think I made it fairly clear that as long as you were around I wouldn't be looking for substitutes.'

'Oh,' said Becky wonderingly. A glow, part unlooked-for delight, part triumph, took hold of her. Tentatively she raised her hand to his face, as she had never dared before. 'Did you mean it?'

'Oh, Becky,' he groaned, cradling her against him fiercely.

Looking up, she saw he was unduly pale, his face pinched with strain, his mouth thinned as if in a self-control excessive even in one of his disciplined habit. He was looking at her anxiously. Slowly, holding his eyes, she began to smile, and standing on tiptoe, she brought his head down to her mouth and kissed him freely.

Charles caught her up hard against him and kissed her until she was breathless, laughing and vitally alive.

When she could speak, she repeated mischievously, 'Did you mean it?'

He held her with hands that shook slightly and his eyes held little flames, but he wasn't prepared to let her tease him without responding in kind. He put his head on one side. 'Oh, I think so,' he allowed, 'at the time.'

Becky recoiled in mock alarm. 'Only at the time?'

He smiled at her very lovingly. 'Oh, what a nagging creature you are! Everything has to be said, doesn't it? Very well, I meant it. At the time and from now on.' He kissed her lightly. 'Always,' he summed up in explanatory tones.

'Ah.' Becky hesitated, running an absorbed finger along the edge of his lapel while Charles watched her in some amusement. At last she made up her mind. 'Does that mean,' she said carefully, 'that I get an engagement ring out of this after all?'

His brows rose. 'I don't follow.'

She glared at him. 'Don't be cantankerous!'

'What on earth——? Try for a little coherence, my child. What are you trying to say?'

'I am trying,' said Becky between her teeth, 'to ask you to marry me.'

'Ah,' said Charles. 'Well, it makes a nice change.' She raised a vengeful hand, which he caught in mid-air. 'I accept,' he said hastily.

For a moment they looked at one another, he laughing openly, she allowing her hand to fall, still clasped in his. She lowered her eyes.

'Thank you,' said Becky meekly. And said nothing else for a very long time.

Have you missed any of these best-selling Harlequin Romances?

By popular demand... to help complete your collection of Harlequin Romances

50 titles listed on the following pages...

Harlequin Reissues

Harlequin Reissues

Complete and mail this coupon today!